'MARVELS

'The nethermost cavern... that see; for their marv... the ground where de... bodied, and evil the m... did Ibn Schacabao say, that happy is the tomb where no wizard hath lain, and happy the town at night whose wizards are all ashes. For it is of old rumour that the soul of the devil-bought hastes not from his charnel clay, but fats and instructs *the very worm that gnaws*; till out of corruption horrid life springs, and the dull scavengers of earth wax crafty to vex it and swell monstrous to plague it. Great holes secretly are digged where earth's pores ought to suffice, and things have learnt to walk that ought to crawl . . .'

ABDUL ALHAZRED –

the *Necronomicon*.

By the same author

The Caller of the Black
Beneath the Moors
The Horror at Oakdene
The Transition of Titus Crow
Spawn of the Winds
The Clock of Dreams
Khai of Ancient Khem
Psychomech
Psychosphere
Psychamok
Ghoul Warning (Poetry)
The Return of the Deep Ones
The House of Cthulhu & Others
In the Moons of Borea
Hero of Dreams
Necroscope
Demogorgon

BRIAN LUMLEY

The Burrowers Beneath

GRAFTON BOOKS

A Division of the Collins Publishing Group

LONDON GLASGOW
TORONTO SYDNEY AUCKLAND

Grafton Books
A Division of the Collins Publishing Group
8 Grafton Street, London W1X 3LA

A Grafton UK Paperback Original 1988

ISBN 0-586-07427-9

Printed and bound in Great Britain by
Collins, Glasgow

Set in Times

This one
with special thanks,
for the memory of August Derleth,
who sanctioned it; and for all those
splendid scriveners of macabre tales
who, over the years, have enlarged
upon or borrowed from the
Cthulhu Mythos
of H. P. Lovecraft.
In so doing, they have helped
to keep the Mythos alive
for the rest of us
to enjoy:

That is not dead which can eternal lie,
And with strange aeons even death may die.

1

The Nethermost Caverns

(From the Files of Titus Crow)

Blowne House
Leonard's-Walk Heath
London
18th May 196–

Ref: – 53/196–
G. K. Lapham & Co.
Head Office, GKL Cuttings
117 Martin Fludd St
Nottingham, Notts.

Dear Mr Lapham,
   Please alter my order as it stands to cover only the most outstanding cases, on which your continued cooperation would be appreciated as ever. This action not to be misconstrued as being all but a cancellation of my custom, on the contrary, but for the time being I would rather you concentrate your efforts on my behalf to *full* coverage of one special line. I require *all* cuttings, one copy of each, from all forty-three dailies normally covered, of current occurrences involving earthquakes, tremors, subsidences, and like phenomena (and back-dated to cover the last three years where at all possible), to continue until further notice. Thank you for your prompt attention.

Yrs faithfully,
T. Crow

Ref: – 55/196–
Edgar Harvey, Esq.
Harvey, Johnson & Harvey, Solicitors
164–7 Mylor Rd
Radcar, Yorks.

Dear Mr Harvey,

I am given to understand that you are the literary agent of Paul Wendy-Smith, the young writer of tales of romantic and/or macabre fiction, and that following his mysterious disappearance in 1933 you became executor to the estate. I was only a very young man at that time, but I seem to remember that because of certain special circumstances publication of the writer's last story (showing, I believe, strange connections with the disappearance of both the author and his uncle, the explorer-archaeologist Sir Amery Wendy-Smith) was held in abeyance. My query is simply this: has the work since seen publication, and if so where may I obtain a copy?

I am, sir, hopefully
expectant of an early
answer, Yrs sincerely,
T. Crow

Harvey, Johnson & Harvey
Mylor Rd
Radcar, Yorks.
22nd May

Blowne House

Dear Mr Crow,

Regarding your inquiry (your reference 55/196– of 19th

May), you are correct, I was executor to the estate of Paul Wendy-Smith – and yes, there was a tale held in abeyance for a number of years until the Wendy-Smiths were both officially pronounced 'missing or dead' in 1937. The story, despite being a very slight piece, has seen publication more recently in an excellently presented and major macabre collection. I enclose proofs of the story, and, should you require the book itself, the publisher's card.

Hoping that this covers your inquiry to your complete satisfaction, I am, Sir,

Yours sincerely,
Edgar Harvey

Blowne House
25th May

Ref: – 58/196–
Features Reporter
Coalville Recorder
77 Leatham St
Coalville, Leics.

My dear Mr Plant,

Having all my life been interested in seismological phenomena, I was profoundly interested in your article in the issue of the *Recorder* for 18th May. I know your coverage was as complete as any man-in-the-street could possibly wish, but wonder if perhaps you could help me in my own rather more specialized inquiry? Tremors of the type you described so well are particularly interesting to me, but there are further details for which, if it is at all possible you can supply them, I would be extremely grateful. Calculations I have made suggest (however inaccurately) that the Coalville shocks were of a linear rather than a general nature; that is, that they occurred on a line almost directly south to north and in that chronological order – the most southerly occurring first. This, at least, is my guess, and I would be grateful if you could corroborate, or (as no doubt the case will be) deny my suspicion; to which end I enclose a stamped, addressed envelope.

Sincerely and appreciatively
Yrs, I am, sir,
Titus Crow

Blowne House
25th May

Ref: – 57/196–
Raymond Bentham, Esq.
3 Easton Crescent
Alston, Cumberland

My dear sir,

Having read a cutting from a copy of the *Northern Daily Mail* for 18th May, I would like to say how vastly interested I was in that article which contained certain parts of your report on the condition of the west sections of Harden Mine's old workings, and feel it a great pity that Sir David Betteridge, scientific adviser to the North-east Coal-Board, has chosen to look at your report in so unenlightened and frivolous a manner.

To me, while admittedly knowing little of yourself or your job, it would seem rather irresponsible on the part of so large and well-founded an industrial board to employ for twenty years an Inspector of Mines without, during that time, discovering that his 'faculties are not all that they should be!'

Now, I am not a young man myself, indeed at sixty-three years of age I am far and away your senior, but I have complete faith in *my* faculties – and, since reading certain of the things in your report which I can (in a rather peculiar way) corroborate, I am also sure that you were *quite correct* in the observations you made in the complex of the discontinued Harden workings. Just how I can be so sure must, unfortunately, remain my secret – like most men I am averse to derision, a point I am sure you will appreciate – but I hope to offer you at least some proof of my sincerity in writing this letter.

Thus, to reassure you beyond any doubt that I am not simply 'pulling your leg', or in any way trying to add my own sarcastic comment to what has already been made of your report, I return your attention to the following:

Other than mentioning briefly certain *outlines* which you say you found etched in the walls of those new and inexplicable tunnels which you discovered down there cut (or rather 'burned', as you had it) through the rock a mile below the surface, you seem reluctant to describe in detail the content or actual forms of those outlines. Might I suggest that this is because you did not wish to be further ridiculed, which you feared might well be the case should you actually describe the etchings? And might I further *tell* you what you saw on those unknown tunnel walls; that those oddly dimensioned designs depicted living creatures of sorts – like elongated octopuses or squids but without recognizable heads or eyes – tentacled worms in fact but of gigantic size?

Dare I lay my cards on the table yet more fully and mention the *noises* you say you heard down there in the depths of the Earth; sounds which were not in any way the normal stress noises of a pit, even given that the mine in question had not been worked for five years and was in poor repair? You said *chanting*, Mr Bentham, but quickly retracted your statement when a certain reporter became unnecessarily facetious. Nonetheless, I take you at your original word: you *said* chanting, and I am sure you meant what you said! How do I know? Again, I am not at liberty to disclose my sources; however, I would be obliged for your reaction to the following:

Ce'haiie ep-ngh fl'hur G'harne fhtagn,
Ce'haiie fhtagn ngh Shudde-M'ell.
Hai G'harne orr'e ep fl'hur,
Shudde-M'ell ican-icanicas fl'hur orr'e G'harne.

Restricted as I am at this time regarding further illuminating my interest in the case, or even explaining the origin of my knowledge of it, but still in the hope of an early answer and perhaps a more detailed account of what you encountered underground, I am, Sir,

Yrs sincerely,
Titus Crow

Coalville Recorder
Coalville, Leics.
28th May

Blowne House

Dear Mr Crow,
    In answer to your 58/196–, of the 25th:
    The tremors that shook Coalville, Leics., on the afternoon of the 17th, were, as you correctly deduced, of a linear nature. (And yes, they did occur south heading north; have in fact continued, or so I believe, farther up-country.) As you are no doubt aware, Coalville is central in an area of expanding mining operations, and doubtless the collapse of old diggings was responsible, in this area

at least, for the peculiar shocks. They lasted from 4:30 until 8:00 P.M., but were not particularly severe – though, I am told, they had a very bad effect on certain inmates of the local Thornelee Sanatorium.

There were, too, other slight surface subsidences, not nearly so bad, almost a year ago. At about that time also, five miners were lost in the collapse of a very narrow and unproductive seam which they were working. The twin brother of one of these men was in a different part of the mine at the time, and much sensational publicity was given his subsequent condition. I did *not* cover his case, though it was done up pretty distastefully in a hack contemporary of the *Recorder* under the heading: 'Siamese Mining Horror!' Apparently the living twin went stark staring mad at the very instant his brother and the other four men were killed!

You should be interested in a series of articles which I am at present planning for the *Recorder*, 'A History of the Midlands Pits', to be published later this year, and I would be pleased to send you the various chapters as they appear if you so desire.

Yours faithfully,
William Plant

Alston, Cumberland
28th May

Blowne House
Dear Mr Crow,

I got your letter yesterday afternoon, and not being much of a writing man, I'm not sure how to answer it, or even if I can find the right words.

First off, let me say you are quite right about the pictures on the tunnel walls – and also about the chanting. How you could know about these things I can't possibly imagine! So far as I know, I'm the only one to have been down that shaft since they closed the pit, and I'm damned if I can think of any other spot on or under the earth where you might have heard sounds like those I heard, or seen drawings the like of them on the tunnel walls. But you obviously have! Those crazy words you wrote down were just like what I heard . . .

Of course, I should have gone down there with a mate, but my No. 2 was off sick at the time and I thought it was going to be just another routine job. Well, as you know, it wasn't!

The reason they asked me to go down and check the old pit out was twofold – I'd worked the seams, all of them, as a youngster and knew my way about, and of course (to hell with what Betteridge says) I am an *Experienced* inspector – but mainly someone had to do the job to see if the empty seams could be propped up or filled in. I imagine that the many subsidences and cave-ins round Ilden and Blackhill have been giving the Coal-Board a bit of a headache of late.

Anyhow, you asked for a more detailed account of what I came up against underground, and I'll try to tell it as it happened. But can I take it that everything I say will be in confidence? See, I have a good pension coming from the Coal-Board in a few years' time, and naturally they don't much care for adverse stuff in the press, particularly stuff to worry local landowners and builders. People don't buy property that's not safe, or ground that's liable to subsidence! And since I've already had one ticking off as it is, well, I don't want to jeopardize my pension, that's all . . .

I think what really annoyed the bosses was when I went on about those tunnels I found down there – not old, timbered seams, mind you, but *tunnels* – round and pretty smoothly finished and certainly artificial. And not just one, as they said in the *Mail*, but half a dozen! A proper maze, it was. Yes, I said those tunnel walls were burned rather than cut, and so they were. At least, that's how they looked, as though they'd somehow been coated on the inside with lava and then allowed to cool!

But there I go running ahead of myself. Better start at the beginning . . .

I went down the main shaft at Harden, using the old emergency lift-cage which they hadn't yet dismantled. There was a gang of lads at the top just in case the old machinery should go on the blink. I wasn't a bit worried, you understand; it's been my job for a long time now and I know all the dangers and what to look for.

I took a budgie down with me in a little cage. I could hang the cage up to the roof timbers while I looked about. There are some of the old-fashioned methods you still can't beat, I reckon. The old-timers used canaries – I took a budgie. That was so I'd know if there was any firedamp down there (methane to you). A heavy gas knocks a bird out in a wink, which lets you know it's time to get out! I wore protective gear and high boots in case of water – Harden's not all that far from the sea, and it's one of the deepest pits in the country. Funny thing, but I *expected* water, yet as it happened I was quite wrong; it was dry as a bone down there. I had a modern lamp on my helmet with a good, powerful beam, and I carried a map of the galleries and seams – standard procedure but hardly necessary in my case.

Well, anyway, I got down the shaft all right and gave the old handset at the bottom a twirl to let the boys on top know that everything was well, and then I set out along the horizontal connecting-shaft to the west-side galleries and coal-seams. Now, you have to understand, Mr Crow, that the main passages are often pretty big things. Some of them are almost as large as any single

15

tube-tunnel in London. I mention this to show that I wasn't shut in, like, or suffering from claustrophobia or anything like that, and it wasn't as if I hadn't been down a pit before – but there was, well, *something*!

It's hard for me to explain on paper like this, but – oh, I don't know – I had this feeling that – it was as if – well, did you ever play hide-and-seek as a child and go into a room where someone was hiding? You can't see him, it's dark, and he's quiet as a mouse, but you know he's in there all the same! That's what it was like down there in that deserted mine. And yet it *was* truly deserted – at that time anyway . . .

Well, I shook this feeling off and went on until I reached the west-side network. This is almost two horizontal miles from the main shaft. Along the way I had seen evidence of deterioration in the timbers, but not enough to explain away the subsidences on the surface. So far as I could see, there had been no actual cave-ins. The place did *stink*, though, like nothing I'd ever smelled before, but it wasn't any sort of gas to affect the budgie or me. Just a very unpleasant smell. Right at the end of the connecting-shaft, at a spot almost directly under Blackhill, I came across the first of the new tunnels. It entered into the shaft from the side away from the sea, and frankly it stopped me dead! I mean, what would *you* have made of it?

It was a hole, horizontal and with hard, regular walls, but it was cut through *solid rock* and not coal! Now, I like to keep slap-up-to-date on mining methods, but I was pretty sure right from the start that this tunnel wasn't dug using any system or machinery I knew of. And yet it seemed I must have missed something somewhere. The thing wasn't shown on my map, though, so in the end I told myself that some new machinery must have been tested down there before they'd closed the mine. I was damned annoyed, I'll tell you – nobody had told me to expect this!

The mouth of the tunnel was about eight feet in diameter, and although the roof wasn't propped up or timbered in any way the bore looked safe-as-houses, solid somehow. I decided to go on down it to see how far it went. It was all of half a mile long, that shaft, Mr Crow; none of it timbered, straight as a die, and the neatest bit of tunnelling work I've seen underground in twenty-five years. Every two hundred yards or so similar tunnels would come in from the sides at right angles, and at three of these junctions there had been heavy falls of rock. This warned me to be careful. Obviously these holes weren't as solid as they looked!

I don't know where the thought came from, but suddenly I found myself thinking of giant moles! I once saw one of these sensational film things about just such animals. Possibly that's where the idea sprang from in my mind. Anyway, I'd no sooner had this thought than I came to a spot where yet another tunnel joined the main one – *but this one came down at an angle from above!*

There was a hole opening into the ceiling, with the edges rounded off and smoothed in some way I don't understand, as if by heat like I said before. Well, I went dead slow from then on, but soon I came out of the tunnel into a big cave. At least, I took it to be a cave, but when I looked closer at the walls I saw that it wasn't! It was simply a junction of a dozen or so of the tunnels. Pillars like stalagmites held up the ceiling. This was where I saw the carvings, those pictures of octopus-things etched in the walls, and I don't think I need add how much *that* put the wind up me!

I didn't hang about there much longer (apart from anything else the stench was terrible), but long enough to check that the place was all of fifty feet across and that the walls were coated or smoothed over with that same sort of lava-stuff. The floor was flat enough but crumbly, almost earthy, and right in the middle of the place I found four great cave-pearls. At least, I *think* they're cave-pearls. They're about four inches across, these things, very hard, heavy, and glossy. Don't ask me how they got down there, I don't know, and I can't see how they might have been formed naturally, like other cave-pearls I remember seeing when I was a kid. Anyway, I put them into a bag I carried and then went back the way I'd come to the terminal of the west-side workings. By then I'd been down there about an hour and a half.

I didn't get far into the actual coal-seams. The first half dozen were down. They had collapsed. But I soon enough found out what had brought them down! In and out of the old workings, lacing them like holes in Gorgonzola, those damned smooth-lined tunnels came and went, literally honeycombing the coal and rock alike! Then, in one of the few remaining old seams that still stood and where some poor-grade coal still remained, I came across yet another funny thing. A tunnel, one of the new ones, had been cut right along the original seam, and I noticed that here the walls weren't of that lava substance but a pitchy, hard tar, exactly the kind of deposit you find bubbling out of hot coal in the coke-ovens, only set as hard as rock . . . !

That was it. I'd had enough, and I set off back towards the main shaft and the lift-cage. It was then I thought I heard the chanting. Thought? – like hell I thought – I *did* hear it; and it was just as you wrote it down! It was distant, seeming to come from a very long way away, like listening to the sea in a shell or hearing a tune you remember in your head . . . But I knew I should never have been hearing things like that down there at all, and I took off for the lift-cage as fast as I could go.

Well, I'll keep the rest of it short, Mr Crow. I've probably said too much already as it is, and I just hope to God that you're not one of those reporter fellows. Still, I wanted to get it off my chest, so what the hell care I?

I finally arrived at the shaft bottom, by which time the chanting had died away, and I gave the lads on top a tinkle on the old handset to haul me up. At the top I made out my report, but not as fully as I've done here, and then I went home . . . I kept the cave-pearls, as mementos if you like, and said nothing about them in my report. I don't see what good they'd be to anyone, anyway. Still, it does seem a bit like stealing. I mean, whatever the things really are – well, they're not mine, are they? I might just send them off anonymously to the museum at Sunderland or Radcar. I suppose the museum people will know what they are . . .

The next morning the reporters came around from the *Daily Mail*. They'd heard I had a bit of a story to tell and pumped me for all I was worth. I had the idea they were laughing at me, though, so I didn't tell them a deal. They must have gone to see old Betteridge when finally they left me – and, well, you know the rest.

And that's it, Mr Crow. If there's something else you'd like to know just drop me another line. Myself, I'd be interested to learn how you come to know so much about it all, and why you want to know more . . .

Yrs sincerely,
R. Bentham

PS

Maybe you heard how they were planning to send two more inspectors down to do the job I'd 'messed up'? Well, they couldn't. Just a few days ago the whole lot fell in! The road between Harden and Blackhill sank ten feet in places, and a couple of brick barns were brought down at Castle-Ilden. There's had to be work done on the walls of the Red Cow Inn in Harden, too, and there have been slight tremors all over the area ever since. Like I said, the mine was rotten with those tunnels down there. I'm only surprised (and thankful!) it held up so long. Oh, and one other thing. I think that the smell I mentioned must, after all, have been produced by a gas of some sort. Certainly my head's been fuzzy ever since. Weak as a kitten, I've been, and damned if I don't keep hearing that awful, droning, chanting sound! All my imagination, of course, for you can take it from me that old Betteridge wasn't even partly right in what he said about me . . .

R.B.

Blowne House
30th May

To: Raymond Bentham, Esq.

Dear Mr Bentham,

I thank you for your prompt reply to my queries of the 25th, and would be obliged if you would give similar keen attention to this further letter. I must of necessity make my note brief (I have many important things to do), but I beg you to have the utmost faith in my directions, strange as they may seem to you, and to carry them out without delay!

You have seen, Mr Bentham, how accurately I described the pictures on the walls of that great unnatural cave in the earth, and how I was able to duplicate on paper the weird chant you heard underground. My dearest wish now is that you remember these previous deductions of mine, and believe me when I tell you *that you have placed yourself in extreme and hideous danger in removing the cave-pearls from the Harden tunnel-complex!* In fact, it is my sincere belief that you are constantly increasing the peril every moment you keep those things!

I ask you to send them to me; I might know what to do with them. I repeat, Mr Bentham, *do not delay but send me the cave-pearls at once*; or, should you decide against it, then for God's sake at least remove them from your house and person! A good suggestion would be for you to drop them back into the shaft at the mine, if that is at all possible; but whichever method you choose in getting rid of them, do it with dispatch! They may rightly be regarded as being infinitely more dangerous than ten times their own weight in nitroglycerin!

Yrs v. truly,
Titus Crow

Blowne House
5 P.M., 30th
May

To: Mr Henri-Laurent de Marigny

Dear Henri,

I've tried to get you on the telephone twice today, only to discover at this late hour that you're in Paris at a sale of antiques! Your housekeeper tells me she doesn't know when you'll be back. I hope it's soon. I may very well need your help! This note will be waiting for you when you get back. *Waste no time, de Marigny, but get round here as soon as you're able!*

Titus

2

Marvels Strange and Terrific

(From the Notebooks of Henri-Laurent de Marigny)

I had known this strange and inexplicable feeling for weeks – a deep-rooted mental *apprehension*, an uneasiness of psyche – and the cumulative effect of this near-indefinable atmosphere of hovering hysteria upon my system, the sheer tautness of my usually sound nerves, was horrible and soul-destroying. I could not for my life fathom whence these brooding fears of things unknown sprang, or even guess at the source of the hideous oppressiveness of air which seemed to hang in tangible heaviness over all my waking and sleeping moments alike, but the combination of the two had been more than sufficient to drive me from London to seek refuge on the Continent.

Ostensibly I had gone to Paris to seek out certain Eastern antiques at the House du Fouche, but when I discovered that my flight to that ancestral city had gained me no respite from my sickening, doom-fraught mood of depression, then I was at a complete loss as to what to do with myself.

In the end, after a stay of only four days, having made one or two small purchases – simply, I suppose, to justify my journey – I determined to return to England.

From the moment my plane touched down in London I felt somehow that I had been *drawn* back from France, and I considered this peculiar prescience proven when, upon arriving at my home, I found Titus Crow's summons waiting for me. His letter had lain on a table in my study, placed there by my housekeeper, for two days; and yet, cryptic as that note was, its message lifted my spirit instantly from the constant gloom it had known for so many weeks, and sent me flying to Blowne House.

It was midafternoon when I reached Crow's sprawling bungalow retreat on the outskirts of the city, and when the leonine occultist opened his door to me I was frankly astonished at the alterations which had taken place in his countenance over the three months since last I had seen him. He was more than tired, that was plain, and his face was drawn and grey. Lines of concentration and worry had etched themselves deep in his high forehead; his broad shoulders were slumped atop his tall, usually energetic frame; his whole aspect betrayed the extensive and sleepless studies to which he must needs have lent himself, making his first words almost unnecessary:

'De Marigny, you got my note! Thank goodness for that! If ever a second head was needed it's now. I've just about knocked myself out with the thing, driven myself to distraction. A clear mind, a fresh approach – By God, it's good to see you!'

Crow ushered me inside, led the way to his study, and there indicated that I should take a seat. Instead I simply stood gazing unbelievingly about the room. My host poured me a customary welcoming glass of brandy before flopping wearily into a chair behind his great desk.

Now, I have said that I gazed unbelievingly about the study: well, let it be understood that Titus Crow's study (incorporating as it does his magnificent occult library), while yet being the apple of his eye, is more often than not the scene of at least a minimal activity, when my friend involves himself within those strange spheres of research which are his speciality; and let it be further understood that I was quite used to seeing the place in less than completely tidy order – but *never* before had I seen anything like the apparent chaos which reigned in that room on this occasion!

Maps, charts, and atlases lay open and in places over-lapping, littering the floor wall to shelved wall, so that I had to step on certain of them to reach a chair; various files, many of them fastened open at marked or paper-clipped places, stood at one end of the cluttered desk and also upon a small occasional table; numbered newspaper cuttings were everywhere, many of them discoloured and plainly faded with age, others very recent; a great note-book, its pages covered top to bottom with careless or hurried scrawlings, lay open at my feet, and rare and commonplace tomes alike on various obscure or little known semimythological, anthropological, and archaeo-logical themes were stacked willy-nilly in one corner of the room at the foot of Crow's great four-handed grand-father clock. The whole was a scene of total disorder, and one that whetted my curiosity to a point where my first astonished outburst sprang as naturally to my lips as might any commonplace inquiry in less bizarre surroundings:

'Titus! What on earth . . . ? You look as though you haven't had a wink of sleep in a week – and the state of this place!' Again I stared about the room, at the apparent disruption of all previous normality.

'Oh, I've been getting my sleep, de Marigny,' Crow answered unconvincingly, 'though admittedly not so much as ordinarily. No, this tiredness of mine is as much a mental as a physical fatigue, I fear. But for heaven's sake, what a *puzzle*, and one that *must* be solved!' He swirled his brandy in its glass, the tired action belying his momen-tarily energetic and forceful mode of expression.

'You know,' I said, satisfied for the moment to let Crow enlighten me in his own time and way, 'I rather fancied someone could use a bit of help, even before I got your note, I mean. I don't know what's been going on, I haven't the faintest inkling what this "puzzle" of yours is, but do you know? Why, this is the first time in weeks that

I've felt at all like tackling anything! I've been under some sort of black cloud, a peculiar mood of despair and strange ennui, and then along came your note.'

Crow looked at me with his head on one side and ruefully smiled. 'Oh? Then I'm sorry, de Marigny, for unless I'm very much mistaken your "peculiar mood of despair" is due to repeat itself in very short order!' His smile disappeared almost immediately. 'But this is nothing frivolous I've got myself into, Henri, no indeed.'

His knuckles whitened as he gripped the arms of his tall chair and leaned forward over the desk. 'De Marigny, if I'm correct in what I suspect, then at this very moment the world is faced with an unthinkable, an unbelievable horror. But *I* believe in it . . . and there were others before me who believed!'

'*Were* others, Titus?' I caught something of the extra weight he had placed on the word. 'Are you alone, then, in this belief of yours?'

'Yes, at least I think I am. Those others I mentioned are . . . no more! I'll try to explain.'

My gaunt-looking friend sat back then and visibly relaxed. He closed his eyes for a second and I knew that he pondered the best way to tell his story. After a few moments, in a quiet and controlled tone of voice, he commenced:

'De Marigny, I'm glad we're two of a kind; I'm damned if I know whom I might confide in if we weren't so close. There *are* others who share this love of ours, this fascination for forbidden things, to be sure, but none I know so well as you, and no one with whom I've shared experiences such as we have known and trembled at together. There's been this thread between us ever since you first arrived in London as a boy, straight off the boat from America. Why! We're even tied by that clock there, once owned by your father!' He indicated the weird, four-handed, strangely ticking monstrosity in the corner. 'Yes, it's as well we're two of a kind, for how could I explain to a stranger the fantastic things I must somehow explain? And even if I could do so without finding myself put away in a padded cell, who would give the thing credit? Even you, my friend, may find it beyond belief.'

'Oh, come now, Titus,' I felt obliged to cut in. 'You couldn't wish for any more inexplicable a thing than that case of the Viking's Stone you dragged me in on! And how about the Mirror of Nitocris, which I've told you of before? What a threat and a horror there! No, it's unfair to doubt a man's loyalty in these things before you've tried it, my friend.'

'I don't doubt your loyalty, Henri – on the contrary – but even so, this thing I've come up against is . . . *fantastic!* There's more than simply the occult involved – if the occult is involved at all – there's myth and legend, dream and fancy, hideous fear and terrifying, well, *survivals!*'

'Survivals?'

'Yes, I think so; but you'll have to let me tell it in my own way. No more interruptions, now. You can question me all you want when I'm done. Agreed?'

I grudgingly nodded my head.

'Survivals, I said, yes,' he then continued. 'Residua of dark and nameless epochs and uncounted cycles of time and existence. Look here; you see this fossil?' He reached into a drawer in his desk and held up an ammonite from the beaches of the Northeast.

'The living creature that this once was dwelt in a warm sea side by side with man's earliest forebears. It was here even before the most antediluvian Adam walked, or crawled, on dry land! But millions of years before that, possibly a forebear of this very fossil itself, *Muensteroceras*, an early ammonite, existed in the seas of the lower

Carboniferous. Now to get back to survivals, Muenstero-ceras had a more mobile and much more highly developed contemporary in those predawn oceans, a fish called Coelacanthus – and yet a *live* coelacanth, its species thought to have been extinct since early Triassic times, was netted off Madagascar in 1938! Then again, though I don't refer specifically to these sorts of things, we have the Loch Ness monster and the alleged giant saurians of Lake Tasek Bera in Malaya – though why such creatures *shouldn't* exist in a world capable of supporting the very real Komodo dragons is beyond me, even if they are thought by many to be pure myth – and even the Yeti and the West German Wald-Schrecken. And there are lesser, absolutely genuine forms, too, plenty of them, come down the ages unaltered by evolution to the present day.

'Now, such as these, real and unreal, are what you might call "survivals", de Marigny, and yet Coelacanthus, "Nessie", and all the others are *geologic infants* in comparison with the things I envisage!'

Here Crow made a pause, getting up to wearily cross the book- and paper-littered floor to pour me another drink, before returning to his desk and continuing his narrative:

'I became aware of these survivals, initially at least, through the medium of dreams; and now I consider that those dreams of mine have been given substance. I've known for a good many years that I'm a highly psychic man; you are of course aware of this as you yourself have similar, though lesser, powers.' (This, from Titus Crow, a statement of high praise!) 'It's only recently, however, that I've come to recognize the fact that these walking "senses" of mine are still at work – more efficiently, in fact – when I'm asleep. Now, de Marigny, unlike that long-vanished friend of your late father's, Randolph Carter, I have never been a great dreamer; and usually

27

my dreams, irregular as they are, are very vague, fragmentary, and the result of late meals and even later hours. Some, though, have been . . . different!

'Well, although this recognition of the extension of my psychic powers even into dreams has come late, I do have a good memory, and fortunately – or perhaps unfortunately, depending how it works out – my memory is supplemented by the fact that as long as I can remember I have faithfully recorded all the dreams I've known of any unusual or vivid content; don't ask me why! Recording things is a trait of occultists, I'm told. But whatever the reason I seem to have written down almost everything of any importance that ever happened to me. And dreams have always fascinated me.' He waved his hand, indicating the clutter on the floor.

'Beneath some of those maps there, you'll find books by Freud, Schrach, Jung, and half a dozen others. Now, the thing that has lately impressed me is this: that all my more *outré* dreams, over a period of some thirty years or more, have occurred simultaneous in time with more serious and far-reaching happenings *in the waking world!*

'Let me give you some examples.' He sorted out an old, slim diary from a dozen or so at one end of his desktop, opening it to a well-turned page.

'In November and December, 1935, I had a recurrent nightmare centring about any number of hideous things. There were winged, faceless bat-things that carried me nightly over fantastic needle-tipped peaks on unending trips towards some strange dimension which I never quite reached. There were weird, ethereal chantings which I've since recognized in the *Cthaat Aquadingen* and which I believe to be part of the *Necronomicon*; terribly deadly stuff, de Marigny! There was a hellish place beyond an alien jungle, a great scabrous circle of rotting earth, in the centre of which a . . . a *Thing* turned endlessly in a bilious green cloak, a cloak alive with a monstrous life all its own. There was madness, utter insanity in the very air! I still haven't deciphered many of the coded sections in the *Cthaat Aquadingen* – and by God I don't intend to! – but those chants I heard in my dreams are delineated there, and heaven knows what they might have been designed to call up!'

'And in the waking world?' I felt bound to ask it, even remembering that I was supposed to bide my time. 'What was going on in the real world throughout this period of strange dreams?'

'Well,' he slowly answered, 'it culminated in certain monstrous occurrences on New Year's Eve at Oakdeene Sanatorium near Glasgow. In fact, five of the inmates died that night in their cells; and a male nurse, too, on a lonely road quite near the sanatorium. The latter was apparently attacked by a beast of some sort . . . torn and horribly chewed! Apart from these deaths, all of them quite inexplicable, one other nurse went mad; and, perhaps most amazing of all, yet five more inmates, previously "hopeless" cases, were later released as perfectly responsible citizens! You can read up on the case from my cuttings-file for that period if you wish . . .

'Now, I'll agree that from what I've told you these occurrences seem to have damn all to do with my dreams; nevertheless, after New Year's Eve, I wasn't bothered again by those dreams!

'And that's not all, for I've checked, and rumour has it that prior to the hellish happenings that night the worst inmates of Oakdeene gave themselves over to some form of mad chanting. And I think I can hazard a guess as to what that chanting was, if not what it was for.

'Anyhow, let's get on.

'Over the next thirty years or so,' Crow continued after closing the first book and taking up a more recent diary,

'I had my share of lesser nightmares – no more than two dozen in all, all of them of course recorded – one of which especially stays in my mind; we'll get on to it in detail in a minute. But in late 1963, commencing on the tenth of November, my sleep was once more savagely invaded, this time by dreams of a vast underwater fortress peopled by things the like of which I never want to see again, in or out of dreams!

'Well, these creatures in their citadel at the bottom of the sea, they were – I don't know – ropy horrors out of the most terrible myths of pre-antiquity, beings without parallel except in the Cthulhu and Yog-Sothoth Cycle. Most of them were preoccupied with some obscure magical – or rather scientific – preparations, assisted in their submarine industry by indescribable blasphemies more heaps of mobile sludge than organic creatures . . . hideously reminiscent of the Shoggoths in the *Necronomicon*, again from the Cthulhu Cycle of myth.

'These Shoggoth-things – I came to think of them as "Sea-Shoggoths" – were obviously subservient to their ropy masters, and yet a number of them stood guard over one certain member of the former beings. I had the mad impression that this . . . this Odd-Thing-Out, as it were – which was, even in its absolute alienage, obviously demented – consisted in fact of a human mind trapped in the body of one of these sea-dwellers!

'Again, during the period through which I experienced these dreams, there were occurrences of peculiarly hideous aspect in the real, waking world. There were awful uprisings in lunatic asylums all over the country, cult gatherings in the Midlands and Northeast, terrible suicides among many members of the "arty set", all coming to a head in the end when Surtsey rose from the sea off the Vestmann Islands on the Atlantic Ridge.

'You know, of course, de Marigny, the basic theme of

30

the Cthulhu Cycle of myth; that at a time yet to come Lord Cthulhu will rise from his slimy seat at Deep R'lyeh in the sea to reclaim his dry-land dominions? Well, the whole thing was horribly frightening, and for a long time I morbidly collected cuttings and articles dealing with Surtsey's rising. Nothing further occurred, however, and Surtsey eventually cooled from its volcanic state into a new island, barren of life but still strangely enigmatic. I have a feeling, Henri, that Surtsey was only the first step, that those ropy things of my dreams are in fact real and that they had planned to raise to the surface whole chains of islands and oddly-dimensioned cities – lands drowned back in the dim mists of Earth's antiquity – in the commencement of a concerted attack on universal sanity . . . an attack led by loathly Lord Cthulhu, his "brothers", and their minions, which once reigned here where men reign now.'

As my friend talked, from his very first mention of the Cthulhu Cycle of myth, I had put to use an odd ability of mine: the power of simultaneous concentration in many directions. One part of my mind I had turned to the absorption of all that Crow was telling me; another followed different tracks. For I knew far more of the Cthulhu Cycle than my gaunt and work-weary friend suspected. Indeed, since suffering certain experiences when, for a brief time, I had owned the accursed Mirror of Queen Nitocris, I had spent much of my time in correlating the legends and pre-human myths surrounding Cthulhu and his contemporaries in the immemorially handed-down records.

Among such 'forbidden' books, I had read the unsuppressed sections of the British Museum's photostat *Pnakotic Manuscript*, allegedly a fragmentary record of a lost 'Great Race', prehistoric even in prehistory; similarly reproduced pages from the *R'lyeh Text*, supposedly written by certain minions of Great Cthulhu himself; the *Unaussprechlichen Kulten* of Von Junzt and my own copy of Ludwig Prinn's *De Vermis Mysteriis*, both in vastly expurgated editions; the Comte d'Erlette's *Cultes des Goules* and Feery's often fanciful *Notes on the Necronomicon*; the hideously revealing and yet disquietingly vague *Revelations of Glaaki*; and those uncoded sections of Titus Crow's priceless copy of the *Cthaat Aquadingen*.

I had learned, somewhat sceptically, of the forces or deities of the unthinkably ancient mythology; of the benign Elder Gods, peacefully palaced in Orion but ever aware of the struggle between the races of Earth and the Forces of Evil; of those evil deities themselves, the Great Old Ones, ruled over by (created by, originating from?) the blind idiot god Azathoth, 'the Bubbler at the Hub', an amorphous blight of nethermost, nuclear confusion from which all infinity radiates; of Yog-Sothoth, 'the all-in-one and one-in-all', coexistent with all time and conterminous in all space; of Nyarlathotep the Messenger; of Great Cthulhu, 'dweller in the Depths' in his House at R'lyeh; of Hastur the Unspeakable, a prime elemental of interstellar space and air, half-brother to Cthulhu; and of Shub-Niggurath, 'the black goat of the woods with a thousand young', fertility symbol in the cycle.

There were, too, other creatures and beings – such as Dagon, fish-god of the Philistines and Phoenicians, ruler over the Deep Ones, ally and servant to Cthulhu; the Tind'losi Hounds; Yibb-Tstll, Nyogtha, and Tsathoggua; Lloigor, Zhar, and Ithaqua; Shudde-M'ell, Glaaki, and Daoloth – many, many of them. Of some of these beings much was made in the mythos, and they were given ample space in the books. Others were more obscure, rarely mentioned, and then only in a vague and indecisive manner.

Basically the legend was this: that in an epoch so remote

in the past as to make Crow's 'geologic infants' statement perfectly acceptable, the Elder Gods had punished a rebellion of the Great Old Ones by banishing them to their various prisoning environs – Hastur to the Lake of Hali in Carcosa; Cthulhu to R'lyeh beneath the Pacific Ocean; Ithaqua to dwell above the ice-wastes of the Arctic; Azathoth, Yog-Sothoth, and Yibb-Tstll to chaotic continua *outside* the geometric design of which the known infinite forms but one surface; Tsathoggua to cthonian Hyperborean burrows, and similarly Shudde-M'ell to other lost labyrinths beneath the earth – so that only Nyarlathotep the Messenger was left free and unprisoned. For in their infinite wisdom and mercy the Elder Gods had left Nyarlathotep alone that he might yet ply the currents between the spheres and carry, one to the other in the loneliness of their banishment, the words of all the evicted forces of evil.

Various magical sigils, signs, and barriers kept the Great Old Ones imprisoned, had done so since time immemorial (again an inadequate cliché), and the books, particularly the *Necronomicon* of the mad Arab, Abdul Alhazred, warned against the removal of such signs and of possible attempts by deluded or 'possessed' mortals to reinstate the Great Old Ones as lords of their former domains. The legend in its entirety was a fascinating thing; but as with all the world's other, greater primal fantasies, it could only be regarded as pure myth, with nothing in it to impress any but the most naïve souls of the possible actuality of its surmises and suggestions. So I still thought, despite certain things Crow had told me in the past and others I had stumbled across myself.

All these thoughts passed in very short order through my head, but thanks to my ability to give many things my full, simultaneous concentration, I missed none of Titus Crow's narrative regarding his dreams of over thirty years and their implications as applied to actual occurrences in the real, waking world. He had covered certain monstrous dreams of a time some years gone, when his nightmares had been paralleled in life by any number of disastrous losses of oceangoing gas- and oil-drilling rigs, and was now about to relate the details of yet more hideous nightmares he had known at a time only some few weeks ago.

'But first we'll go back to those dreams I skipped over earlier,' he said, as I banished all other pictures from my mind. 'The reason I did that was because I didn't want to bore you with duplication. You see, they first came to me as long ago as August, 1933, and though they were not so detailed they were more or less the same as my most recent, recurrent nightmares. Yes, those dreams, until recently, have been coming nightly, and if I describe one of them, then I shall have described most of them. A few have been different!

'To make it short, Henri, I have been dreaming of subterranean beings, octopus-things apparently without heads or eyes, creatures capable of organic tunnelling through the deepest buried rocks with as little effort as hot knives slicing butter! I don't know for sure yet just what they are, these burrowers beneath; though I'm pretty certain they're of an hitherto unguessed species as opposed to creatures of the so-called "supernatural", survivors of a time before time rather than beings of occult dimensions. No, I can only guess, but my guess is that they represent an unholy horror! And if I'm correct, then, as I've already said, the whole world is in hellish danger!'

Crow closed his eyes, leaned back in his chair, and put his fingertips up to his furrowed forehead. Plainly he had said as much as he was going to without prompting. And yet I found myself no longer truly eager to question him.

This was, without a doubt, a much different Titus Crow from the man I had known previously. I full knew the extent of his probing into various strange matters, and that his research over the years in the more obscure corners of various sciences had been prodigious, but had his work finally proved too much for him?

I was still worriedly staring at him in sympathetic apprehension when he opened his eyes. Before I could hide it, he saw the expression on my face and smiled as I tried to cover my embarrassment.

'I . . . I'm sorry, Titus, I – '

'What was it you said, de Marigny?' He stopped me short. 'Something about doubting a man before trying him? I told you it was going to be hard to swallow, but I don't really blame you for whatever doubts you have. I *do* have proof, though, of sorts . . .'

'Titus, please forgive me,' I answered dejectedly. 'It's just that you look so, well, tired and washed out. But come on – proof, you said! What sort of proof do you mean?'

He opened his desk drawer again, this time to take out a folder of letters, a manuscript, and a square cardboard box. 'First the letters,' he said, handing me the slim folder, 'then the manuscript. Read them, de Marigny, while I doze, and then you'll be able to judge for yourself when I show you what's in the box. Then, too, you'll be better able to understand. Agreed?'

I nodded, took a long sip at my brandy, and began to read. The letters I managed pretty quickly; they drew few conclusions in themselves. Then came the manuscript.

3

Cement Surroundings

(Being the Manuscript of Paul Wendy-Smith)

1

It will never fail to amaze me how certain allegedly Christian people take a perverse delight in the misfortunes of others. Just how true this is was brought forcibly home to me by the totally unnecessary whispers and rumours which were put about following the disastrous decline of my closest living relative.

There were those who concluded that just as the moon is responsible for the tides, and in part the slow movement of the Earth's upper crust, so was it also responsible for Sir Amery Wendy-Smith's behaviour on his return from Africa. As proof they pointed out my uncle's sudden fascination for seismography – the study of earthquakes – a subject which so took his fancy that he built his own instrument, a model which does not incorporate the conventional concrete base, to such an exactitude that it measures even the most minute of the deep tremors which are constantly shaking this world. It is that same instrument which sits before me now, rescued from the ruins of the cottage, at which I am given to casting, with increasing frequency, sharp and fearful glances.

Before his disappearance my uncle spent hours, seemingly without purpose, studying the fractional movements of the stylus over the graph.

For my own part I found it more than odd the way in which, while Sir Amery was staying in London after his return, he shunned the underground and would pay extortive taxi fares rather than go down into what he termed 'those black tunnels'. Odd, certainly, but I never considered it a sign of insanity.

Yet even his few really close friends seemed convinced of his madness, blaming it upon his living too close to those dead and nighted nigh-forgotten civilizations which so fascinated him. But how could it have been otherwise? My uncle was both antiquarian and archaeologist. His strange wanderings to foreign lands were not the result of any longing for personal gain or acclaim. Rather were they undertaken out of a love of the life; for any fame which resulted – as frequently occurred – was more often than not shrugged off on to the ever-willing personages of his colleagues.

They envied him, those so-called contemporaries of his, and would have emulated his successes had they possessed the foresight and inquisitiveness with which he was so singularly gifted – or, as I have now come to believe, with which he was cursed. My bitterness towards them is directed by the way in which they cut him after the dreadful culmination of that last, fatal expedition. In earlier years many of them had been 'made' by his discoveries, but on that last trip those hangers-on had been the uninvited, the ones out of favour, to whom he would not offer the opportunity of fresh, stolen glory. I believe that for the greater part their assurances of his insanity were nothing more than a spiteful means of belittling his genius.

Certainly that last safari was his *physical* end. He who before had been straight and strong, for a man his age, with jet hair and a constant smile, was now seen to walk with a pronounced stoop and had lost a lot of weight. His hair had greyed and his smile had become rare and nervous while a distinct tic jerked the flesh at the corner of his mouth.

Before these awful deteriorations made it possible for his erstwhile 'friends' to ridicule him, before the expedition, Sir Amery had deciphered or translated (I know little of these things) a handful of decaying, centuried shards known in archaeological circles as the *G'harne Fragments*. Though he would never fully discuss his findings I knew it was that which he learned which sent him, ill-fated, into Africa.

He and a handful of personal friends, all equally learned gentlemen, ventured into the interior seeking a legendary city which Sir Amery believed had existed centuries before the foundations were cut for the pyramids. Indeed, according to his calculations, Man's primal ancestors were not yet conceived when G'harne's towering ramparts first reared their monolithic sculptings to predawn skies. Nor with regard to the age of the place, if it existed at all, could my uncle's claims be disproved; new tests on the *G'harne Fragments* had shown them to be pre-Triassic, and their very existence, in any form other than centuried dust, was impossible to explain.

It was Sir Amery, alone and in a terrible condition, who staggered upon an encampment of savages five weeks after setting out from the native village where the expedition had last had contact with civilization. No doubt the ferocious men who found him would have done away with him there and then but for their superstitions. His wild appearance and the strange tongue in which he screamed, plus the fact that he had emerged from an area which was taboo in their tribal legends, stayed their hands. Eventually they nursed him back to a semblance of health and conveyed him to a more civilized region whence he was slowly able to make his way back to the outside world. Of the expedition's other members nothing has since been seen or heard. Only I know the story, having read it in the letter my uncle left me, but more of that later . . .

Following his lone return to England, Sir Amery developed those eccentricities already mentioned, and the merest hint or speculation on the part of outsiders with reference to the disappearance of his colleagues was sufficient to start him raving horribly of such inexplicable things as 'a buried land where Shudde-M'ell broods and bubbles, plotting the destruction of the human race and the release from his watery prison of Great Cthulhu . . .' When he was asked *officially* to account for his missing companions, he said that they had died in an earthquake; and though, reputedly, he was asked to clarify his answer, he would say no more.

Thus, being uncertain as to how he would *react* to questions about his expedition, I was loath to ask him of it. However, on those rare occasions when he saw fit to talk of it without prompting, I listened avidly; for I, as much if not more so than others, was eager to have the mystery cleared up.

He had been back only a few months when he suddenly left London and invited me up to his cottage, isolated here on the Yorkshire Moors, to keep him company. This invitation was a thing strange in itself, as he was one who had spent months in absolute solitude in various far-flung desolate places and liked to think of himself as something of a hermit. I accepted, for I saw the perfect chance to get a little of that peaceful quiet which I find particularly beneficial to my writing.

One day, shortly after I had settled in, Sir Amery showed me a pair of strangely beautiful pearly spheres. They measured about four inches in diameter, and, though he had been unable to positively identify the material from which they were made, he was able to say that it appeared to be some unknown combination of calcium, chrysolite, and diamond-dust. *How* the things had been made was, as he put it, 'anybody's guess'. The spheres, he told me, had been found at the site of the dead G'harne – the first intimation he had offered that he had actually found the place – buried beneath the earth in a lidless stone box which had borne upon its queerly angled sides certain utterly alien engravings. Sir Amery was anything but explicit with regard to those designs, merely stating that they were so loathsome in what they suggested that it would not do to describe them too closely. Finally, in answer to my probing questions, he told me that they depicted monstrous sacrifices to some unthinkable cthonian deity. More he refused to say but directed me, since I seemed 'so damnably eager', to the works of Commodus and the hag-ridden Caracalla.

He mentioned that also upon the box, along with the pictures, were many lines of sharply cut characters much similar to the cuneiform and dot-group etchings of the *G'harne Fragments* and, in certain aspects, having a disturbing likeness to the almost unfathomable *Pnakotic Manuscript*. Quite possibly, he went on, the container had been a toy-box of sorts and the spheres, in all probability, were once the baubles of a child of the ancient city; certainly children, or young ones, were mentioned in what he had managed to decipher of the odd writing on the box.

It was during this stage of his narrative that I noticed Sir Amery's eyes were beginning to glaze over and his speech was starting to falter, almost as though some strange psychic block were affecting his memory. Without warning, like a man suddenly gone into an hypnotic trance, he began muttering of Shudde-M'ell and Cthulhu, Yog-Sothoth and Yibb-Tstll – 'alien *Gods* defying description' – and of mythological places with equally fantastic names: Sarnath and Hyperborea, R'lyeh and Ephiroth, and many more.

Eager though I was to learn more of that tragic expedition, I fear it was I who stopped Sir Amery from staying on. Try as I might, on hearing him babbling so, I could not keep a look of pity and concern from showing on my face which, when he saw it, caused him to hurriedly excuse himself and flee to the privacy of his room. Later, when I looked in at his door, he was engrossed with his seismograph and appeared to be relating the markings on its graph to an atlas of the world which he had taken from his shelves. I was concerned to note that he was quietly arguing with himself.

Naturally, being what he was and having such a great interest in peculiar ethnic problems, my uncle had always possessed, along with his historical and archaeological source books, a smattering of works concerning elder-lore and primitive, doubtful religions. I mean such works as *The Golden Bough* and Miss Murray's *Witch Cult*. But what was I to make of those *other* books which I found in his library within a few days of my arrival? On his shelves were at least nine works which I knew were so outrageous in what they suggest that they have been mentioned by widely differing authorities over a period of many years as being damnable, blasphemous, abhorrent, unspeakable, literary lunacy. These included the *Cthaat Aquadingen* by an unknown author, Feery's *Notes on the Necronomicon*, the *Liber Miraculorem*, Eliphas Lévi's *History of Magic*, and a faded, leather-bound copy of the hideous *Cultes des Goules*. Perhaps the worst thing I saw was a slim volume by Commodus which that 'Blood Maniac' had written in 183 A.D. and which was protected by lamination from further fragmentation.

And moreover, as if these books were not puzzling and disturbing enough, there was that other thing . . .

What of the indescribable droning *chant* which I often heard issuing from Sir Amery's room in the dead of night? This first occurred on the sixth night I spent with him, when I was roused from my own uneasy slumbers by the morbid accents of a language it seemed impossible for the vocal cords of man to emulate. Yet my uncle was weirdly fluent with it, and I scribbled down an oft-repeated sentence-sequence in what I considered the nearest written approximation of the spoken words I could find. These words – or at least *sounds* – were:

> Ce'haaie ep-ngh fl'hur G'harne fhtagn,
> Ce'haaie fhtagn ngh Shudde-M'ell.
> Hai G'harne orr'e ep fl'hur,
> Shudde-M'ell ican-icanicas fl'hur orr'e G'harne.

Though at the time I found the thing impossible to pronounce as I heard it, I have since found that with each passing day, oddly, the pronunciation of those lines becomes easier – as if with the approach of some obscene horror I grow more capable of expressing myself in that horror's terms. Perhaps it is just that lately in my dreams, I have found occasion to mouth those very words, and, as all things are far simpler in dreams, my fluency has passed over into my waking hours.

But that does not explain the tremors – the same inexplicable tremors which so terrorized my uncle. Are the shocks which cause the ever-present quiverings of the seismograph stylus merely the traces of some vast, subterrene cataclysm a thousand miles deep and five thousand miles away – *or are they caused by something else?* Something so *outré* and fearsome that my mind freezes when I am tempted to study the problem too closely.

3

There came a time, after I had been with him for a number of weeks, when it seemed plain that Sir Amery was rapidly recovering. True, he still retained his stoop, though to me it seemed no longer so pronounced, and his so-called 'eccentricities', but he was more his old self in other ways. The nervous tic had left his face completely and his cheeks had regained something of their former colour. His improvement, I conjectured, had much to do with his never-ending studies of the seismograph; for I had established by that time that there was a definite connection between the measurements of that machine and my uncle's illness. Nevertheless, I was at a loss to understand why the internal movements of the Earth should so determine the state of his nerves. It was after a trip to his room, to look at that instrument, that he told me more of dead G'harne. It was a subject I should have attempted to steer him away from.

'The fragments,' he said, 'told the location of a city the name of which, G'harne, is known only in legend and which has in the past been spoken of on a par with Atlantis, Mù, and R'lyeh. A myth and nothing more. But if you give a legend a concrete location you strengthen it somewhat – and if that location yields up something of the past, centuried relics of a civilization lost for aeons, then the legend becomes history. You'd be surprised how much of the world's history has in fact been built up that way.

'It was my hope, a hunch you might call it, that G'harne had been real; and with the deciphering of the fragments I found it within my power to *prove*, one way or the other, G'harne's elder existence. I have been in some strange places, Paul, and have listened to even stranger stories. I once lived with an African tribe whose people declared they knew the secrets of the lost city, and their storytellers told me of a land where the sun never shines; where Shudde-M'ell, hiding deep in the honeycombed ground, plots the dissemination of evil and madness throughout the world and plans the resurrection of other, even worse abominations!

'He hides there in the ground and awaits the time when the stars will be *right*, when his horrible hordes will be sufficient in number, and when he can infest the entire world with his loathsomeness and bring about the return of those others more loathsome yet!

'I was told stories of fabulous star-born creatures who inhabited the Earth millions of years before Man appeared, who were still here, in certain dark places, when he eventually evolved. I tell you, Paul' – his voice rose – '*that they are here even now – in places undreamed-of!* I was told of sacrifices to Yog-Sothoth and Yibb-Tstll that would make your blood run cold, and of weird rites practised beneath prehistoric skies before Old Khem was born. These things I've heard make the works of Albertus Magnus and Grobert seem tame; De Sade himself would have paled at the hearing.'

My uncle's voice had been speeding up progressively with each sentence, but now he paused for breath and in a more normal tone and at a reduced rate he continued:

'My first thought on deciphering the fragments was of an expedition. I may tell you I had learned of certain things I could have dug for here in England – you'd be surprised what lurks beneath the surface of some of those peaceful Cotswold hills – but that would have alerted a host of so-called "experts" and amateurs alike, and so I decided upon G'harne. When I first mentioned an expedition to Kyle and Gordon and the others I must surely have produced quite a convincing argument, for they all insisted upon coming along. Some of them, though, I'm sure, must have considered themselves upon a wild-goose chase. As I've explained, G'harne lies in the same realm as Mu or Ephiroth – or at least it did – and they must have seen themselves as questing after a veritable Lamp of Aladdin; but despite all that they came. They could hardly afford *not* to come, for if G'harne was real . . . why! Think of the lost glory! They would never have forgiven themselves. And that's why I can't forgive *myself*. But for my meddling with the *G'harne Fragments* they'd all be here now, God help them . . .'

Again Sir Amery's voice had become full of some dread excitement, and feverishly he continued:

'Heavens, but this place sickens me! I can't stand it much longer. It's all this grass and soil. Makes me shudder! Cement surroundings are what I need – and the thicker the cement the better! Yet even the cities have their drawbacks . . . undergrounds and things. Did you ever see Pickman's *Subway Accident*, Paul? By God, what a picture! And that night . . . that *night*!

'If you could have *seen* them – coming up out of the diggings! If you could have felt the tremors – The very ground rocked and danced as they rose! We'd disturbed them, do you see? They may have even thought they were under attack, and up they came. My God! What could

45

have been the reason for such *ferocity*? Only a few hours before I had been congratulating myself on finding the spheres, and then . . . and then – '

Now he was panting and his eyes, as before, had partly glazed over; his voice, too, had undergone a strange change of timbre and his accents were slurred and alien.

'*Ce'haiie, ce'haiie* – the city may be buried but whoever named the place *dead* G'harne didn't know the half of it. *They were alive!* They've been alive for millions of years; perhaps they can't die . . . ! And why shouldn't that be? They're gods, aren't they, of a sort? Up they come in the night – '

'Uncle, please!' I interrupted.

'You needn't look at me so, Paul,' he snapped, 'or think what you're thinking either. There's stranger things happened, believe me. Wilmarth of Miskatonic could crack a few yarns, I'll be bound! You haven't read what Johansen wrote! Dear Lord, *read the Johansen narrative!*

'*Hai, ep fl'hur* . . . Wilmarth . . . the old babbler . . . What is it he knows that he won't tell? Why was that which was found at those Mountains of Madness so hushed up, eh? What did Pabodie's equipment draw up out of the earth? Tell me those things, if you can! Ha, ha, ha! *Ce'haiie, ce'haiie – G'harne icanicas* . . .'

Shrieking now and glassy-eyed he stood, with his hands gesticulating wildly in the air. I do not think he saw me at all, or anything – except, in his mind's eye, a horrible recurrence of what he imagined had been. I took hold of his arm to calm him but he brushed my hand away, seemingly without knowing what he was doing.

'Up they come, the rubbery things . . . Good-bye, Gordon . . . Don't scream so – the shrieking turns my mind – but it's only a dream. A nightmare like all the others I've been having lately. It *is* a dream, isn't it? Good-bye Scott, Kyle, Leslie . . .'

Suddenly, eyes bulging, he spun wildly around. '*The ground is breaking up! So many of them . . . I'm falling!*

'It's not a dream – dear God! *It's not a dream!*

'No! Keep off, do you hear? Aghhh! *The slime . . .* got to run! Run! Away from those – voices? – away from the sucking sounds and the chanting . . .'

Without warning he suddenly broke into a chant himself, and the awful *sound* of it, no longer distorted by distance or the thickness of a stout door, would have sent a more timid listener into a faint. It was similar to what I had heard before in the night and the words do not seem so evil on paper, almost ludicrous in fact, but to hear them issuing from the mouth of my own flesh and blood – and with such unnatural fluency:

> 'Ep, ep-eeth, fl'hur G'harne
> G'harne fhtagn Shudde-M'ell hyas Negg'h.'

While chanting these incredible mouthings Sir Amery's feet had started to pump up and down in a grotesque parody of running. Suddenly he screamed anew and with startling abruptness leaped past me and ran full tilt into the wall. The shock knocked him off his feet and he collapsed in a heap on the floor.

I was worried that my meagre ministrations might not be adequate, but to my immense relief he regained consciousness a few minutes later. Shakily he assured me that he was 'all right, just shook up a bit', and, supported by my arm, he retired to his room.

That night I found it impossible to close my eyes. I wrapped myself in a blanket instead, and sat outside my uncle's room to be on hand if he were disturbed in his sleep. He passed a quiet night, however, and paradoxically enough, in the morning, he seemed to have got the thing out of his system and was positively improved.

Modern doctors have known for a long time that in certain mental conditions a cure may be obtained by inciting the patient to relive the events which caused his illness. Perhaps my uncle's outburst of the previous night had served the same purpose – or at least, so I thought, for by that time I had worked out new ideas regarding his abnormal behaviour. I reasoned that if he had been having recurrent nightmares and had been in the middle of one on that fateful night of the earthquake, when his friends and colleagues were killed, it was only natural that his mind should become temporarily – even permanently – unhinged upon awakening and discovering the carnage. And if my theory were correct, it also explained his seismic obsessions . . .

4

A week later came another grim reminder of Sir Amery's condition. He had seemed so much improved. though he still occasionally rambled in his sleep, and had gone out into the garden 'to do a bit of trimming'. It was well into September and quite chilly, but the sun was shining and he spent the entire morning working with a rake and hedge-clippers. We were doing for ourselves and I was just thinking about preparing the midday meal when a singular thing happened. I distinctly felt the ground *move* fractionally under my feet and heard a low rumble.

I was sitting in the living room when it happened, and the next moment the door to the garden burst open and my uncle rushed in. His face was deathly white and his eyes bulged horribly as he fled past me to his room. I was so stunned by his wild appearance that I had barely moved from my chair by the time he shakily came back into the room. His hands trembled as he lowered himself into an easy chair.

'It was the ground . . . I thought for a minute that the ground . . .' He was mumbling, more to himself than to me, and visibly trembling from head to toe as the after-effect of the shock hit him. Then he saw the concern on my face and tried to calm himself.

'The ground, Paul, I was sure I felt a tremor – but I was mistaken. It must be this place. All this open space. The moors. I fear I'll really have to make an effort and get away from here. There's altogether too much soil and not enough cement! Cement surroundings are the thing . . .'

I had had it on the tip of my tongue to say that I too had felt the shock, but upon learning that he now believed himself mistaken I kept quiet. I did not wish to needlessly add to his already considerable disorders.

That night, after Sir Amery had retired, I went through into his study – a room which, though he had never said so, I knew he considered inviolate – to have a look at the seismograph. Before I looked at the machine, however, I saw the notes spread out upon the table beside it. A glance was sufficient to tell me that the sheets of white foolscap were covered with fragmentary jottings in my uncle's heavy handwriting, and when I looked closer I was sickened to discover that they were a rambling jumble of seemingly disassociated – yet apparently *linked* – occurrences connected in some way with his weird delusions. These notes have since been delivered permanently into my possession and are as reproduced here:

HADRIAN'S WALL.
122–128 A.D. Limestone Bank. (Gn'yah of the *G'harne Fragments?*) Earth tremors interrupted the diggings, which is why cut basalt blocks were left in the uncompleted ditch with wedge-holes ready for splitting.

W'nyal Shash. (MITHRAS?)

The Romans had their own deities – *but it wasn't Mithras* that the disciples of Commodus, the Blood Maniac, sacrificed to at Limestone Bank! And that was the same spot where, fifty years earlier, a great block of stone was unearthed and discovered to be covered with *inscriptions and engraven pictures!* Silvanus the Centurion defaced it and buried it again. A skeleton, positively identified as Silvanus' by the signet ring on one of its fingers, has been lately found *beneath the ground* (deep) where once stood a Vicus Tavern at Housesteads Fort – but we don't know *how* he vanished! Nor were Commodus' followers any too careful. According to Atullus and Caracalla they also vanished overnight – *during an earthquake!*

AVEBURY.

(Neolithic A'byy of the *G'harne Fragments* and *Pnakotic Manuscript???*) Reference Stukeley's book, *A Temple to the British Druids* – incredible! Druids, indeed! But Stukeley was pretty close when he said snake worship! *Worms, more like it!*

COUNCIL OF NANTES. (9th Century.)

The Council didn't know what it was doing when it ordered: 'Let the *stones* also which, deceived by the derision of the *demons*, they worship amid ruins and in wooded places, where they both make their vows and bestow their offerings, be *dug up* from the very foundations, and let them be cast into such places as never will their devotees be able to find them again . . .' I've read that paragraph so many times that it's become imprinted upon my mind! *God only knows what happened to the poor devils who tried to carry out the Council's orders . . . !*

DESTRUCTION OF GREAT STONES.

In the 13th and 14th Centuries the Church also attempted the removal of certain stones from Avebury, because of *local superstitions* which caused the country folk to take part in *heathen worship* and *witchcraft* around them! In fact some of the stones *were* destroyed – by fire and douching – 'because of the *devices* upon them'.

INCIDENT.

1320–25. Why was a big effort made to bury one of the great stones at Avebury? An *earth tremor* caused the stone to slip, trapping a workman. *No effort appears to have been made to free him . . . !* The 'accident' happened at dusk and two other men *died of fright!* Why? And why did other diggers flee the scene? And what was the titanic *Thing* which one of them saw

50

wriggling away into the ground? Allegedly there was a smell . . .
By their SMELL shall ye know them . . . Was it a member of
another nest of the timeless ghouls?

THE OBELISK.

Why was the so-called Stukeley Obelisk broken up? The pieces
were buried in the early 18th Century but in 1833 Henry Browne
found burned sacrifices at the site . . . and nearby, at Silbury
Hill . . . *My God! That devil-mound!* There are some things,
even amid these horrors, which don't bear thinking of – and
while I've still got my sanity Silbury Hill had better remain one
of them!

AMERICA: INNSMOUTH.

1928. What actually happened and why did the Federal Government drop depth-charges off Devil Reef in the Atlantic coast
just out of Innsmouth? Why were half Innsmouth's citizens
banished – *and where to?* What was the connection with Polynesia and what also lies buried in the lands *beneath the sea?*

WIND WALKER.

(Death-Walker, Ithaqua, Wendigo, etc.) Yet *another* horror –
though of a different type! And such *evidence!* Alleged human
sacrifices in Manitoba. Unbelievable circumstances surrounding
Norris Case! Spencer of Quebec University literally *affirmed* the
validity of the case . . . and at . . .

But that is as far as the notes go, and when first I read
them I was glad that such was the case. It was quickly
becoming all too apparent that my uncle was far from well
and still not quite right in his mind. Of course, there was
always the chance that he had written those notes before
his seeming improvement, in which case his plight was not
necessarily as bad as it appeared.

Having put the notes back exactly as I found them, I
turned my attention to the seismograph. The line on the
graph was straight and true, and when I dismantled the
spool and checked the chart I saw that it had followed
that almost unnaturally unbroken smoothness for the last
twelve days. As I have said, that machine and my uncle's
condition were directly related, and this proof of the
quietness of the Earth was undoubtedly the reason for his

comparative well-being of late. But here was yet another oddity: Frankly I was astonished at my findings, for I was certain I had felt a tremor – indeed I had *heard* a low rumble – and it seemed impossible that both Sir Amery and myself should suffer the same, simultaneous sensory illusion.

I rewound the spool and then, as I turned to leave the room, I noticed that which my uncle had missed. It was a small brass screw lying on the floor. Once more I unwound the spool to find the countersunk hole which I *had* noticed before but which had not made an impression of any importance upon my mind. Now I guessed that it was meant to house that screw. I am nothing where mechanics are concerned and could not tell what part that small component played in the workings of the machine; nevertheless I replaced it and again set the instrument in order. I stood then, for a moment, to ensure that everything was working correctly and for a few seconds noticed nothing abnormal. It was my ears which first warned of the change. There had been a low, clockwork hum and a steady, sharp scraping noise before. The hum was still attendant, but in place of the scraping sound was a jerky scratching which drew my fascinated eyes to the stylus.

That small screw had evidently made all the difference in the world. No wonder the shock we had felt in the afternoon, which had so disturbed my uncle, had gone unrecorded. The instrument had not been working correctly then – *but now it was!*

Now it could plainly be seen that every few minutes the ground was being shaken by tremors which, though they were not so severe as to be felt, were certainly strong enough to cause the stylus to wildly zigzag over the surface of the revolving graph paper . . .

I felt in a far more shaken state than the ground when I finally retired that night. Yet I could not readily decide the cause of my nervousness. Just why should I feel so apprehensive about my discovery? True, I knew that the effect of the now – correctly? – working machine upon my uncle would probably be unpleasant, might even cause another of his 'outbursts'; but was that knowledge alone sufficient to unsettle me? On reflection I could see no reason whatever why any particular area of the country should receive more than its usual quota of earth tremors.

Eventually I concluded that the machine was either totally at fault or simply far too sensitive – perhaps the brass screw needed adjustment – and so finally I went to sleep assuring myself that the strong shock we had felt had been merely coincidental to my uncle's condition. Still, I noticed before I dozed off that the very air itself seemed charged with a strange tension, and that the slight breeze which had wafted the late leaves during the day had gone completely, leaving in its passing an absolute quiet in which, during my slumbers, I fancied all night that the ground trembled beneath my bed . . .

5

The next morning I was up early. I was short of writing materials and had decided to catch the lone morning bus into Radcar. I left the cottage before Sir Amery was awake, and during the journey I thought back on the events of the previous day and decided to do a little research while I was in town. In Radcar I had a bite to eat before calling at the offices of the *Radcar Mirror* where a Mr McKinnen, a sub-editor, was particularly helpful. He spent some time on the office telephones making extensive inquiries on my behalf. Eventually I was told that for the better part of a year there had been no tremors of any importance in England, a point I must obviously have challenged had not further information been forthcoming. I learned that there *had* been some minor shocks and that these had occurred at places as close as Goole, a few miles away (that one within the last forty-eight hours), and as far as Tenterden near Dover. There had also been a very minor tremor at Ramsey in Huntingdonshire. I thanked Mr McKinnen profusely for his help and would have left then but, as an afterthought, he asked me if I would be interested in checking through the paper's international files. I gratefully accepted and was left on my own to study a great pile of interesting translations. Of course, as I expected, most of the information was useless to me, but it did not take me long to sort out what I was after.

At first I had difficulty in believing the evidence of my own eyes. I read that in August there had been quakes in Aisne of such severity that one or two houses had collapsed and a number of people had been injured. These shocks had been likened to those of a few weeks earlier at Agen in that they seemed to be caused more by some *settling of the ground* than by actual tremors. In early July there had also been shocks in Calahorra, Chinchon, and Ronda in Spain. The trail went as straight as the flight of an arrow and lay across – *or rather under* – the straits of Gibraltar to Xauen in Spanish Morocco, where an entire neighbourhood of houses had collapsed. Farther yet, to . . . But I had had enough; I dared look no more; I did not wish to know – not even remotely – the whereabouts of dead G'harne . . .

Oh! I had seen more than sufficient to make me forget about my original errand. My book could wait, for now there were more important things to do. My next port of call was the town library, where I took down Nicheljohn's *World Atlas* and turned to that page with a large, folding map of the British Isles. My geography and knowledge of England's counties are passable, and I had noticed what I considered to be an oddity in the seemingly unconnected places where England had suffered those 'minor quakes'. I was not mistaken. Using a second book as a straight edge I lined up Goole in Yorkshire and Tenterden on the south coast and saw, with a tingle of monstrous foreboding, that the line passed very close to, if not directly through, Ramsey in Huntingdonshire. With dread curiosity I followed the line north and, through suddenly fevered eyes, saw that it passed *within only a mile or so of the cottage on the moors!*

With unfeeling, rubbery fingers I turned more pages, until I found the leaf showing France. For a long moment I paused – then I fumblingly found Spain and finally Africa. For a long while I just sat there in numbed silence, occasionally turning the pages, automatically checking names and localities.

My thoughts were in a terrible turmoil when I eventually left the library, and I could feel upon my spine the chill, hopping feet of some abysmal dread from the beginning of time. My previously wholesome nervous system had already started to crumble.

During the journey back across the moors in the evening bus, the drone of the engine lulled me into a kind of half-sleep in which I heard again something Sir Amery had mentioned – something he had murmured aloud while sleeping and presumably dreaming. He had said: 'They don't like water . . . England is safe . . . have to go too deep . . .'

The memory of those words shocked me back to wakefulness and filled me with a further icy chill which got into the very marrow of my bones. Nor were these feelings of horrid foreboding misleading, for awaiting me at the cottage was that which went far to completing the destruction of my entire nervous system.

As the bus came around the final wooded bend which hid the cottage from sight – *I saw it!* The place had collapsed! I simply could not take it in. Even knowing all I did – with all my slowly accumulating evidence – it was too much for my tortured mind to comprehend. I left the bus and waited until it had threaded its way through the parked police cars and others of curious travellers before crossing the road. The fence to the cottage had been knocked down to allow an ambulance to park in the now queerly *tilted* garden. Spotlights had been set up, for it was almost dark, and a team of rescuers toiled frantically at the incredible ruins. As I stood there, aghast, I was approached by a police officer. Having stumblingly identified myself, I was told the following story.

A passing motorist had actually seen the collapse; the tremors attendant had been felt in nearby Marske. The motorist, realizing there was little he could do on his own, had driven on at speed into Marske to report the thing and bring help. Allegedly the house had gone down like a pack of cards. The police and the ambulance had been on the scene within minutes and rescue operations had begun immediately. Up to now it appeared that my uncle had been out when the collapse occurred, for as of yet there had been no trace of him. There *had* been a strange, poisonous odour about the place but this had vanished soon after the rescue work had started. The floors of all the rooms except the study had now been cleared, and during the time it took the officer to bring me up-to-date even more debris was being frantically hauled away.

Suddenly there was a lull in the excited babble of voices. I saw that the sweating rescue workers were standing amid the ruins in a gang looking down at something. My heart gave a wild leap and I scrambled over the debris to see what they had found.

There, where the floor of the study had been, was that which I had feared and more than half expected. It was simply a hole. A gaping hole in the floor – *but from the angles at which the floorboards lay, and the manner in which they were scattered about, it looked as though the ground, rather than sinking, had been pushed up from below . . .*

6

Nothing has since been seen or heard of Sir Amery Wendy-Smith, and though he is listed as being *missing*, I know that in fact he is dead. He is gone to worlds of ancient wonder and my only prayer is that his soul wanders on *our* side of the threshold. For in our ignorance we did Sir Amery a great injustice – I and all the others who thought he was out of his mind – all of us. Each of his queer ways, I understand them all now, but the understanding has come hard and will cost me dear. No, he was not mad. He did the things he did out of self-preservation, and though his precautions came to nothing in the end, it was fear of a nameless evil and not madness which prompted them.

But the worst is still to come. I myself have yet to face a similar end. I know it, for no matter what I do the tremors haunt me. Or is it only in my mind? No, there is little wrong with my mind. My nerves may be gone but my mind is intact. I *know* too much! *They* have visited me in dreams, as I believe *they* must have visited my uncle, and what *they* have read in my mind has warned *them* of *their* danger. *They* dare not allow me further to investigate, for it is just such meddling which may one day fully reveal *them* to men – *before they are ready!*

God! Why hasn't that folklorist fool Wilmarth at Miskatonic answered my telegrams? There must be a way out! Even now *they* dig – those dwellers in darkness . . .

But no – this is no good! I must get a grip on myself and finish this narrative. I have not had time to tell the authorities the truth, but even if I had I know what the result would have been. 'There's something wrong with all the Wendy-Smith blood,' they would say. But this manuscript will tell the story for me and will also stand as a warning to others. Perhaps when it is seen how my *passing* so closely parallels that of Sir Amery, people will be curious; with this manuscript to guide them perhaps men will seek out and destroy Earth's elder madness before it destroys them . . .

A few days after the collapse of the cottage on the moors, I settled here in this house on the outskirts of Marske to be close at hand if – though I could see little hope of it – my uncle should turn up again. But now some dread power keeps me here. I *cannot* flee . . . At first *their* power was not so strong, but now . . . I am no longer able even to leave this desk, and I know that the end must be coming fast. I am rooted to this chair as if grown here and it is as much as I can do to type!

But I must . . . I must . . . And the ground movements are much stronger now. That hellish, damnable, mocking stylus – leaping so crazily over the paper!

I had been here only two days when the police delivered to me a dirty, soil-stained envelope. It had been found in the ruins of the cottage – near the lip of that curious hole – and was addressed to me. It contained those notes I have already copied and a letter from Sir Amery which, if its awful ending is anything to go on, he must have just finished writing when the horror came for him. When I consider, it is not surprising that the envelope survived the collapse; *they* would not have known what it was, and so would have had no interest in it. Nothing in the cottage seems to have been deliberately damaged – nothing *inanimate*, that is – and so far as I have been able to discover the only missing items are those terrible spheres, *or what remained of them!*

But I must hurry. I cannot escape and all the time the tremors are increasing in strength and frequency. No! I will not have time. No time to write all I intended to say. The shocks are too heavy . . . to o heav y. Int erfer in g with my t ypi ng. I will finis h this i n th e only way rem ain ing to me and staple S ir Amer y's lett er to th is man usc rip t no w.

Dear Paul,

In the event of this letter ever getting to you, there are certain things I must ask you to do for the safety and sanity of the world. It is absolutely necessary that these things be explored and *dealt with* – though how that may be done I am at a loss to say. It was my intention, for the sake of my own sanity, to forget what happened at G'harne. I was wrong to try to hide it. At this very moment there are men digging in strange, forbidden places, and who knows what they may unearth? Certainly all these horrors must be tracked down and rooted out – but not by bumbling amateurs. It must be done by men who are ready for the ultimate in hideous, cosmic horror. Men with weapons. Perhaps flamethrowers would do the trick . . . Certainly a scientific knowledge of war would be a necessity . . . Devices could be made to track the enemy . . . I mean specialized seismological instruments. If I had the time I would prepare a dossier, detailed and explicit, but it appears that this letter will have to suffice as a guide to tomorrow's horror-hunters.

You see, *I now know for sure that they are after me* – and there's nothing I can do about it! It's too late! At first even I, just like so many others, believed myself to be just a little bit mad. I refused to admit to myself that what I had *seen* happen had ever happened at all! To admit that was to admit *complete* lunacy – but it was real, all right, it did happen – *and will again!*

Heaven only knows what's been wrong with my seismograph, but the damn thing's let me down in the worst possible way! Oh, *they* would have got me eventually, but I might at least have had time to prepare a proper warning.

I ask you to think, Paul . . . Think of what has happened at the cottage . . . I can write of it as though it had already happened – because I know *it must! It will!* It is Shudde-M'ell, come for his spheres . . .

Paul, look at the manner of my death, for if you are reading this then I am either dead or disappeared – which means the same thing. Read the enclosed notes carefully, I beg you. I haven't the time to be more explicit, but these notes of mine should be of some help. If you are only half so inquiring as I believe you to be, you will surely soon come to recognize a fantastic horror which, I repeat, the whole world must be *made* to believe in . . . The ground is really shaking now but, knowing that it is the end, I am steady in my horror . . . Not that I expect my present calm state of mind to last. I think that by the time *they* actually come for me my mind will have snapped completely. I can imagine it now. The floor splintering, erupting, to admit *them*. Why! Even thinking of it my senses recoil at the terror of the thought. There will be a hideous *smell*, a *slime*, a *chanting* and gigantic *writhing* and . . . and then –

Unable to escape I await the thing. I am trapped by the same hypnotic power that claimed the others at G'harne. What monstrous memories! How I awoke to see my friends and companions sucked dry of their life's blood by wormy, vampirish *things* from the cesspools of time! Gods of alien dimensions! I was hypnotized then by this same terrible force, unable to move to the aid of my friends or even to save myself!

Miraculously, with the passing of the moon behind some wisps of cloud, the hynotic effect was broken. Then, screaming and sobbing, utterly broken, temporarily out of my mind, I fled, hearing behind me the droning, demoniac chanting of Shudde-M'ell and his hordes.

Not knowing that I did it, in my mindlessness I carried with me those hell-spheres . . . Last night I dreamed of them. And in my dreams I saw again the inscriptions on that stone box. Moreover, *I could read them!*

All the fears and *ambitions* of those hellish things were there to be read as clearly as the headlines in a daily newspaper! 'Gods' they may or may not be but one thing is sure: the greatest setback to their plans for the conquest of Earth *is their terribly long and complicated reproductive cycle!* Only a handful of young are born every thousand years; but, considering how *long* they have been here, the time must be drawing ever nearer when their numbers will be *sufficient!* Naturally, this tedious buildup of their numbers makes them loath to lose even a single member of their hideous spawn – *and that is why they have tunnelled these many thousands of miles, even under deep oceans, to retrieve the spheres!*

I had wondered why they should be following me – and now I know. I also know *how!* Can you not guess how they know where I am, Paul, or why they are coming? Those spheres are like a beacon to them; a siren voice calling. *And just as any other parent – though more out of awful ambition, I fear, than any type of emotion we could understand – they are merely answering the call of their young!*

But they are too late!

A few minutes ago, just before I began this letter, the things hatched! Who would have guessed that they were eggs – or that the container I found them in *was an incubator?* I can't blame myself for not knowing it; I even tried to have the spheres X-rayed once, damn them, but they reflected the rays! And the shells were so thick! Yet at the time of hatching those same shells just splintered into tiny fragments. The creatures inside were no bigger than walnuts. Taking into account the sheer *size* of an adult they must have a fantastic growth rate. Not that those two will ever grow! I shrivelled them with a cigar . . . *and you should have heard the mental screams from those beneath!*

If only I could have known earlier, *definitely*, that it was not madness, then there might have been a way to escape this horror. But no use now. My notes – look into them, Paul, and do what I ought to have done. Complete a detailed dossier and present it to the authorities. Wilmarth may help, and perhaps Spencer of Quebec University. Haven't much time now. *Cracks in ceiling.*

That last shock – ceiling coming away in chunks – the floor – coming up! Heaven help me, they're coming up. I can feel them groping inside my mind as they come –

Sir,

Reference this manuscript found in the ruins of 17 Anwick

Street, Marske, Yorkshire, following the earth tremors of September this year and believed to be a 'fantasy' which the writer, Paul Wendy-Smith, had completed for publication. It is more than possible that the so-called disappearance of both Sir Amery Wendy-Smith and his nephew, the writer, were nothing more than promotion stunts for this story: it is well-known that Sir Amery is/was interested in seismography and perhaps some prior intimation of the two quakes supplied the inspiration for his nephew's tale. Investigations continuing.

Sgt J. Williams
Yorks County Constabulary
2nd October 1933

4

Cursed the Ground

(From de Marigny's Notebooks)

It soon became obvious that the occultist, despite his
denials, was far more tired than he admitted, for he did
in fact doze, closing his eyes and drowsing, breathing
deep and rhythmically where he sat in his chair, while I
read the letters and the – fantasy? – of Paul Wendy-
Smith.

I admit quite frankly that when I was finished with that
document my mind was in something of a whirl! There
had been so many factual references in the supposed
'fiction', and why had the author deliberately chosen to
give his characters his own, his uncle's, and many another
once-living person's names? Considering the letters I had
read prior to this disturbing document, the conviction was
rapidly growing in me that Crow's assertions – so far at
least – stood proven. For while my friend had not directly
said so, nevertheless I could guess that he believed the
Wendy-Smith manuscript to be nothing less than a statement of fantastic fact!

When I had properly done with my reading, and while
I checked over again the contents of certain of the letters,
Crow still nodded in his chair. I rustled the papers noisily
as I put them down on his desk and coughed politely.
These sudden sounds brought my friend back in an instant
to full consciousness.

There were many things for which I would have liked
explanations; however, I made no immediate comment
but remained intently alert and thoughtful as Crow stirred
himself to pass me the box containing . . . what?

I believed I already knew.

I carefully removed the cardboard lid, noting that my guess had been correct, and lifted out one of the four beautifully lustrous spheres the box contained.

'The spawn of Shudde-M'ell,' I quietly commented, placing the box back on the desk and examining the sphere in my hand. 'The eggs of one of the lesser known deities of the Cthulhu Cycle of myth. Bentham did send them to you, then, as you requested?'

He nodded an affirmative. 'But there was no letter with the box, and it seemed pretty hastily or clumsily wrapped to me. I believe I must have frightened Bentham pretty badly . . . or at least, *something* did!'

Frowning, I shook my head, doubt suddenly inundating my mind once more. 'But it's all so difficult to believe, Titus, and for a number of reasons.'

'Good!' he instantly replied. 'In resolving your own incredulity, which I intend to do, I might also allay the few remaining doubts which I myself yet entertain. It *is* a difficult thing to believe, Henri – I've admitted that – but we certainly can't afford to ignore it. Anyhow, what reasons were you speaking of just now, when you voiced your reluctance to accept the thing as it stands?'

'Well for one thing' – I sat back in my chair – 'couldn't the whole rigmarole *really* be a hoax of some sort? Wendy-Smith himself hints of just such a subterfuge in that last paragraph of his, the "police report".'

'Ah!' he exclaimed. 'A good point, that – but I've already checked, Henri, and that last paragraph was *not* part of the original manuscript! It was added by the author's publisher, a clever extract from an actual police report on the disappearances.'

'Then what about this Bentham chap?' I persisted. 'Couldn't he have read the story somewhere? Might he not simply be adding his own fancies to what he considers an intriguing mystery? He has, after all, admitted to a certain interest in weird and science-fiction cinema. Perhaps his taste also runs to macabre literature! It's possible, Titus. The Wendy-Smith story may, as you seem to suspect, be based on fact – may indeed have been drawn from life, a veritable diary, as the continuing absence of Sir Amery and his nephew after all these years might seem to demand – but it *has* seen print as a fiction!'

I could see that he considered my argument for a moment, but then he said: 'Do you know the story of "The Boy Who Cried Wolf", Henri? Of course you do. Well, I've a feeling that Paul Wendy-Smith's last manuscript was dealt with on a similar principle. He had written a fair number of macabre stories, you see, and I'm afraid his agent and executor – despite some preliminary doubts, as witness the delay in publishing – finally saw this last work as just another fiction. It puts me disturbingly in mind of the Ambrose Bierce case. You know the circumstances to which I refer, don't you?'

'Hmmm?' I murmured, frowning as I wondered what he was getting at. 'Bierce? Yes. He was an American master of the macabre, wasn't he? Died in 1914 . . .?'

'Not "died", Henri,' he quickly corrected me. 'He simply disappeared, and his disappearance was quite as mysterious as anything in his stories – quite as final as the vanishment of the Wendy-Smiths!'

He got down on his hands and knees on the floor and began to collect up some of the books and maps. 'But in any case, my friend, you've either not been listening to me as well as you might, or' – he smiled up at me – 'you have very little faith in what I've sworn to be the truth. I'm talking about my dreams, Henri – think about my dreams!'

He gave me time to consider this, then said, 'But there, just supposing that by some freak those nightmares of mine were purely coincidental; and suppose further that

Mr Bentham is, as you suggest, "a hoaxer". How do you explain away these eggs? You think perhaps that Bentham, who appears to be a reasonably down-to-earth Northeasterner, went down to his workshop and simply put them together, out of a bucket or two of common-or-garden chrysolite and diamond-dust? No, Henri, it won't wash. Besides' – he stood up and took one of the things from the box, weighing it carefully in his hand – 'I've checked them out. So far as I can determine they're the real thing, all right. In fact *I know they are!* I've had little time to test them as fully as I would like to, true, but one thing is sure – they do defy X-rays! Very strange when you consider that while they're undeniably heavy there doesn't appear to be any lead in their makeup. And something else, something far more definite . . .'

He put down the egg, neatly stacked the books and papers earlier picked up from the floor, and returned to his chair. From the centre drawer in his desk he took a certain surgical instrument. 'This was lent to me by a neighbour friend of mine, that same friend who tried to radiograph the eggs for me. Care to eavesdrop, de Marigny?'

'A stethoscope?' I took the thing wonderingly from him. 'You mean – ?'

'This was something Sir Amery missed,' Crow cut me off. 'He had the right idea with his earthquake-detector – I've decided, by the way, to obtain a seismograph as soon as possible – but he might have tried listening for small things as well as big ones! But no, that's being unfair, for of course he didn't know until the end just what his pearly spheres were. In trying the stethoscope test I was really only following his lead, on a smaller scale. Well, go on,' he demanded again as I hesitated. 'Listen to them!'

I fitted the receivers to my ears and gingerly touched the sensor to one of the eggs, then held it there more firmly. I imagine the rapid change in my expression was that which made Crow grin in that grim fashion of his. Certainly, in any situation less serious, I might have expected him to laugh. I was first astounded, then horrified!

'My God!' I said after a moment, a shudder hurrying down my spine. 'There are – *fumblings!*'

'Yes,' he answered as I sat there, shaken to my roots, 'there are. The first stirrings of life, Henri, a life undreamed-of – except, perhaps, by an unfortunate few – from beyond the dim mists of time and from behind millennia of myth. A race of creatures unparalleled in zoology or zoological literature, indeed entirely *unknown*, except in the most doubtful and obscure tomes. But they're real, as real as this conversation of ours.'

I felt an abrupt nausea and put the egg quickly back into its box, hurriedly wiping my hands on a kerchief from my pocket. Then I shakily passed the stethoscope back across the desk to my friend.

'They have to be destroyed.' My voice cracked a little as I spoke. 'And without delay!'

'Oh? And how do you think Shudde-M'ell, his brothers and sisters – if indeed they are bisexual – would react to that?' Crow quietly asked.

'What?' I gasped, as the implications behind his words hit me. 'You mean that already – '

'Oh, yes.' He anticipated my question. 'The parent creatures know where their eggs are, all right. They have a system of communication better than anything we've got, Henri. Telepathy I imagine. That was how those other, earlier eggs were traced to Sir Amery's cottage on the moors; that was how they were able to follow him home through something like four thousand miles of subterrene burrows! Think of it, de Marigny. What a task they set themselves – to regain possession of the stolen eggs – and by God, they almost carried it off, too! No, I daren't destroy them. Sir Amery tried that, remember? And what happened to him?'

After a slight pause, Crow continued: 'But, having given Sir Amery's portion of the Wendy-Smith papers a lot of thought, I've decided that he could only have been partly right in his calculations. Look at it this way: certainly, if as Wendy-Smith deduced the reproductive system of Shudde-M'ell and his kind is so long and tedious, the creatures couldn't allow the loss of two future members of their race. But I'm sure there was more than merely that in their coming to England. Perhaps they'd had it planned for a long time – for centuries maybe, even aeons! The way I see it, the larceny of the eggs from G'harne finally prodded the burrowers into early activity. Now, we know they came out of Africa – to recover their eggs, for revenge, whatever – *but we have no proof at all that they ever went back!*'

'Of course,' I whispered, leaning forward to put my elbows on the desk, my eyes widening in dawning understanding. 'In fact, at the moment, all the evidence lies in favour of the very reverse!'

'Exactly,' Crow agreed. 'These things are on the move, Henri, and who knows how many of their nests there may be, or where those nests are? We know there's a burrow in the Midlands, at least I greatly suspect it, and another at Harden in the Northeast – but there could be dozens of others! Don't forget Sir Amery's words: ". . . he waits for the time when he can infest *the entire world* with his loathsomeness . . ." And for all we know this invasion of 1933 may not have been the first! What of Sir Amery's notes, those references to Hadrian's Wall and Avebury? Yet more nests, Henri?'

He paused, momentarily lost for words, I suspected.

By then I was on my feet, pacing to and fro across that

part of the floor Crow had cleared. And yet . . . Once more I found myself puzzled. Something Crow had said . . . My mind had not had time yet to adjust to the afternoon's revelations.

'Titus,' I finally said, 'what do you mean by "a Midlands nest"? I mean, I can see that there is some sort of horror at Harden, but what makes you think there may be one in the Midlands?'

'Ah! I see that there's a point you've missed,' he told me. 'But that's understandable for you haven't yet had all the facts. Now listen: Bentham took the eggs on the seventeenth of May, Henri, and later that same day, Coalville, two hundred miles away, suffered those linear shocks heading in a direction from south to north. I see it like this: a number of members of the Midlands nest had come up close to the surface – where the earth, not being so closely packed, is naturally easier for them to navigate – and had set off to investigate this disturbance of the nest at Harden. If you line up Harden and Coalville on a map – as I have done, again taking my lead from the Wendy-Smith document – you'll find that they lie almost directly north and south! But all this in its turn tells us something else' – he grew excited – 'something I myself had missed until just now – there are no adults of the species "in residence", as it were, at Harden! These four Harden eggs were to form the nucleus of a new conclave!'

He let this last sink in, then continued: 'Anyhow, this Coalville . . . *expedition*, if you like, arrived beneath Harden on or about the twenty-sixth of the month, causing that collapse of the mine which Bentham commented upon. There, discovering the eggs to be missing, "abducted", I suppose you could say, the creatures picked up the mental trail towards Bentham's place at Alston.'

He paused here to sort out a newspaper cutting from a small pile on his desk and passed it across for my inspection. 'As you can see, Henri, there were tremors at Stenhope, County Durham, on the twenty-eighth. Need I point out that Stenhope lies directly between Harden and Alston?'

I flopped down again in my chair and helped myself liberally to Crow's brandy.

'Titus, it's plain you can't keep the eggs here!' I told him. 'Heavens, why even now – unseen, unheard, except perhaps as deep tremors on some meteorologist's machinery – these underground octopuses, these subterranean vampires might be on their way here, burning their way through the bowels of the earth! You've put yourself in as much danger as Bentham before he sent you the eggs!'

Then, suddenly, I had an idea. I leaned forward to thump the table. 'The sea!' I cried.

Crow appeared startled by my outburst. 'Eh?' he asked. 'What do you mean, "the sea", de Marigny?'

'Why, that's it!' I slapped a clenched fist into the palm of my hand. 'No need to destroy the eggs and risk the revenge of the adult creatures – simply take them out to sea and drop them overboard! Didn't Sir Amery say that they fear water?'

'It's an idea,' Crow slowly answered, 'and yet – '

'Well?'

'Well, I had it in my mind to use the eggs differently, Henri. To use them more *constructively*, I mean.'

'Use them?'

'We have to put a stop to Shudde-M'ell once and for all, my friend, and we have the key right here in our hands!' He tapped the box with a fingernail. 'If only I could conceive a plan, a system that might work, discover a way to put paid to the things for good. But for that I need time, which means hanging on to the eggs, and that in turn means – '

'Titus, wait,' I rudely interrupted, holding up my hands.

There was something in the back of my mind, something demanding concentration. Abruptly it came to me and I snapped my fingers. 'Of course! I knew there was something bothering me. Now, correct me if I go wrong, but surely we've decided that this Shudde-M'ell creature and his kind feature in the Cthulhu Cycle?'

'Yes.' My friend nodded, obviously at a loss to decide what I was getting at.

'It's simply this,' I said. 'How come these creatures aren't *prisoned*, as their hideous brothers and cousins were in the mythology by the Elder Gods untold millions of years ago?'

I had a point. Crow frowned, quickly moving out from his desk and crossing the room to take from a bookshelf his copy of Feery's *Notes on the Necronomicon*.

'This will do for now,' he said, 'at least until I can get it fixed for you to check through the *Necronomicon* itself at the British Museum. And this time we'll have to fix it for you to read the *whole* book! It's a dangerous task, though, Henri. I've read it myself, some time ago, and was obliged to forget most of what I learned – it was that or madness! In fact, I think we'd better limit your research to selected sections from Henrietta Montague's translation. Are you willing to help me in this?'

'Of course, Titus,' I answered. 'Just pass on your orders. I'll carry them out as best I can, you know that.'

'Good, then that's to be your special task in this,' he told me. 'You can save me a lot of time by correlating and summing up the whole Cthulhu Cycle, with special reference to Shudde-M'ell in the mythology. I'll list certain other books which I think might be helpful later. Right now, though, let's see what Feery has to say on it.'

We were hardly to know it at that time, but things were not to be in any way as Crow planned, for events yet to come would surely have confounded *any* plans he might have made. As it was, we could not know this, and so my haggard friend flipped the leaves of Feery's often fanciful reconstruction of Alhazred's dreadful book until he found the page he was looking for.

'Here we are,' he eventually declared, 'the passage entitled: "Ye Power in ye Five-Pointed Star".' He settled himself in his chair and began to read:

'"Armour against Witches & Daemons, Against ye Deep Ones, ye Dools, ye Voormais, ye Tacho-Tacho, ye Mi-Go, ye Shoggaoths, ye Ghasts, ye Valusians, & all such Peoples & Beings that serve ye Great Olde Ones & ye Spawn of Them, lies within ye Five-Pointed Star carven of grey Stone from ancient Mnar; which is less strong against ye Great Olde Ones Themselves. Ye Possessor of ye Stone shall find himself able to command all Beings which creep, swim, crawl, walk, or fly even to ye Source from which there is no returning. In Yhe as in Great R'lyeh, in Y'ha-nthlei as in Yoth, in Yuggoth as in Zothique, in N'kai as in Naa-Hk & K'n-yan, in Carcosa as in G'harne, in ye twin Cities of Ib and Lh-yib, in Kadath in ye Cold Waste as at ye Lake of Hali, it shall have Power; yet even as Stars wane & grow cold, even as Suns die & ye Spaces between Stars grow more wide, so wanes ye Power of all things – of ye Five-Pointed Star-Stone as of ye Spells put upon ye Great Olde Ones by ye benign Elder Gods, & that Time shall come as once was a Time when it shall be known:

That is not dead which can eternal lie,
And with strange Aeons even Death may die."'

'"In Carcosa as in G'harne,"' I repeated when Crow had done. 'Well, there we seem to have it!'

'Yes,' he answered drily, frowning at the open book, 'but I'm pretty sure that this is a different version from the one in the Museum copy of the *Necronomicon*. I wish to God Feery was still alive! I've often pondered his knowledge regarding the *Necronomicon* – to say nothing of many another rare book. Still' – he tapped with his

72

fingernail on the page with the relevant passage – 'there's part of your answer at least.'

'So it appears that Shudde-M'ell *was* prisoned at G'harne.' I frowned. 'Which means that somehow he managed to escape! But how?'

'That's something we may never know. Henri, unless – ' Crow's eyes widened and his face went grey.

'Yes, what is it, Titus?'

'Well,' he slowly answered, 'I have a lot of faith in Alhazred, even in Feery's version. It's a monstrous thought, I know, but nevertheless it's just possible that the answer lies in what I've just read out: ". . . so wanes ye Power of all things – of ye Five-Pointed Star-Stone as of ye Spells put – "'

'Titus!' I cut him off. 'What you're saying is that the spells of the Elder Gods, the power of the pentacle is past – and if that's true . . .'

'I know,' he said. 'I know! It also means that Cthulhu and all the others must likewise be free to roam and kill and . . .'

He shook himself, as if breaking free from some monstrous spider's web, and managed a weak smile. 'But no, that can't be – no, we'd know about it if Cthulhu, Yog-Sothoth, Yibb-Tstll, and all the others were free. We'd have known long ago. The whole world . . .'

'Then how do you explain – '

'I make no attempt to explain anything, Henri,' he brusquely replied. 'I can only hazard guesses. It looks to me as though some years ago, anything up to a century ago, the spells or star-stones – whichever applies in Shudde-M'ell's case – were removed from G'harne by some means or other. Perhaps by accident, or there again, perhaps purposely . . . by persons in the power of the Great Old Ones!'

'Maliciously or inadvertently – by "persons in the power

of the Great Old Ones" – these I can understand,' I said, 'but accidentally? How do you mean, Titus?'

'Why! There are all kinds of natural accidents, Henri. Landslips, floods, volcanic eruptions, earthquakes – natural quakes, I mean – and any single one of them, occurring in the right place, could conceivably carry away the star-stones keeping one or more of these diverse horrors prisoned. This all provided, of course, that in Shudde-M'ell's case star-stones were the only prisoning devices!'

Listening to the occultist my mind suddenly whirled. For a moment I actually felt sick. 'Titus, wait! It's . . . too *fast* for me . . . too fast!' I made a conscious effort to calm myself.

'Look, Titus. My whole concept of things, everything, has turned upside down for me in one afternoon. I mean, I've always had this interest in the occult, the weird, the macabre, anything out of the ordinary, and at times it has been dangerous. Both of us, over the years, have experienced hideous dangers – *but this!* If I admit the existence of Shudde-M'ell – a lesser deity in a mythology which I believed could never exercise over me anything more than a passing interest – which now' – I glanced in loathing fascination at the box on the desk – 'it seems I *must* admit, then I must also believe in the existence of all the other related horrors! Titus, until today the Cthulhu Cycle of myth, granted that I've looked pretty deeply at it, was quite simply *myth*; fascinating and even, yes, dangerous – but only in the way that all occult studies are dangerous! Now –'

'Henri,' Crow cut in. 'Henri, if you feel that this is something you can't accept, the door is open. You're not involved yet, and there's nothing to stop you from keeping out of it. If you do decide, however, that you want to be in on this thing, then you're welcome – but you should know now that it may well be more dangerous than anything you ever came up against before!'

'It's not that I'm afraid, Titus; don't misunderstand,' I told him. 'It's simply the *size* of the concept! I *know* that there are extramundane occurrences, and I've had my share of experiences that can only be described as "supernatural", but they have always been the exception. You are asking me to believe that the Cthulhu Cycle of myth is nothing less than *prehistoric fact* – which means in effect that the very foundation of our entire sphere of existence is built on alien magic! If such is the case then "occult" is normal and Good grew out of Evil, as opposed to the doctrines of the Christian mythos!'

'I refuse to be drawn into a theological argument, Henri,' he answered. 'But that is my basic concept of things, yes. However, let's get one or two points quite clear, my friend. In the first place, for "Magic" read "Science".'

'I don't follow.'

'Brainwashing, Henri! The Elder Gods knew that they could never hope to imprison beings as powerful as the deities of the Cthulhu Cycle behind merely physical bars. They made their prisons *the minds of the Great Old Ones themselves* – perhaps even their bodies! They implanted mental and genetic blocks into the psyches and beings of the forces of evil and all their minions, that at the sight of – or upon sensing the presence of – certain symbols, or upon hearing those symbols reproduced as sound, those forces of evil are held back, impotent! This explains why comparatively simple devices such as the Mnaran starstones are effective, and why, in the event of such stones being removed from their prisoning locations, certain chants or written symbols may still cause the escaped powers to retreat.'

For a moment this explanation mazed me even more than before, but then I suspiciously asked: 'Titus, did you know all of this earlier, or is it just something you've freshly dreamed up?'

'The theory has been my own personal opinion for quite a long while, Henri, and it explains so many hitherto "inexplicable" things. I believe, too, that it is alluded to in a certain somewhat less than cryptic passage in the *Cthaat Aquadingen*. As you know, the book has a short chapter dedicated to "Contacting Cthulhu in Dreams"! Mercifully the actual devices required to perform this monstrously dangerous feat are given only in code – in practically impossible ciphers – and concern themselves in some unknown way with Nyarlathotep. Still, in the same chapter, the author makes a statement very relevant towards proving my own beliefs regarding the Elder Gods as scientists. I have a note here somewhere that I copied for easy reference.' He searched atop his littered desk.

'Ah! Here it is. It has quite definite parallels with much that's rather better known in the Cthulhu Cycle, and certainly seems to lend itself well to the most recent Christian mythos. Anyway, listen:

'"Ye Science as practised by a Majority of ye Prime Ones was & is & always will be that of ye Path of Light, infinitely recognized throughout Time, Space & all ye Angels as beneficent to ye *Great All's* Continuation. Certain of ye Gods, however, of a rebellious Nature, chose to disregard ye Dictums of ye Majority, & in ye constant Gloom of ye Dark Path renounced their immortal Freedom in Infinity & were banished to suitable Places in Space & Time. But even in Banishment ye Dark Gods railed against ye Prime Ones, so that those Followers of ye Light Path must needs shut them *Outside* of all Knowledge, imposing upon their Minds certain Strictures & ye Fear of ye Light Path's Ways, & impressing into their Bodies a Stigma defying Generation; that ye Sins of ye Fathers might be carried down through Eternity & visited upon ye Children & ye Children's children for ever; or until a Time should come as was once, when all Barriers crumble, & ye Stars & Dwellers therein, & ye Spaces between ye Stars & Dwellers therein, & all Time &

Angels & Dwellers therein be falsely guided into ye ultimate Night of ye Dark Path – until ye *Great All* close in & become One, & Azathoth come in His golden Glory, & Infinity begin again . . ."'

Crow paused at the end of his reading before saying, 'There's quite a bit that's obviously not relevant, of course, but in the main I believe – '

'Why didn't you tell me all this when I first arrived today?' I cut him off.

'You weren't ready for it, my friend.' He grinned mirthlessly. 'You're hardly ready now!'

I gave the matter some more thought. 'Then what you're really saying is that there is no such thing as the supernatural?'

'Correct!'

'But you've so often used the word, and recently, in its recognized context.'

'Purely out of habit, Henri, and because *your* concept of existence still admits its use – will do for some time, as will my own – until we get used to the idea.'

I mulled the matter over. 'The magic of the Elder Gods was a sort of psychiatric science,' I mused. 'You know, Titus, I can far easier face an alien concept than a supernatural one. Why! It all breaks down quite simply to this: that the combined forces of evil, the Great Old Ones, are nothing more than alien beings or forces against which it will be necessary to employ alien weapons.'

'Well, yes, basically. We shall have to fight these things with the weapons left us by the Elder Gods. With chants and incantations – scientifically implanted mental and genetic blocks – with the power of the pentacle, but mainly with the knowledge that they are *not* supernatural but simply *outside* forces.'

'But wait,' I still countered. 'What of the, well, "supernatural" occurrences, in all their various forms, which we've encountered in the past? Did they, too, spring from – '

'Yes, Henri, I have to believe they did. *All* such occurrences have their roots in the olden science of the Elder Gods, in a time before time. Now, how do you say, de Marigny – are you with me or – ?'

'Yes,' I answered without further hesitation; and I stood up to firmly grasp his outstretched hand across his great desk.

5

Evil the Mind

(From de Marigny's Notebooks)

I did not get away from Blowne House until very late that
night, but at least I had an idea (for some reason still
more than somewhat vague) of the task before me. Crow
had not gone lightly on me, on the contrary, he had
always been a hard taskmaster, but I knew that on this
occasion he had taken by far the majority of the work
upon his own shoulders. As it happened, I was never to
commence work on that portion of the overall task
appointed to me; it would be pointless therefore to set it
down in detail.

This aside, then, we had worked out a system, apparently foolproof in its simplicity, whereby Shudde-M'ell
(or whichever of his brood led the English nests) would
be given more than a hard time, indeed an *impossible*
time, retrieving the four Harden eggs. Crow had written
three letters to trusted friends of his. One to an ancient
and extremely eccentric recluse living in Stornoway in the
Hebrides; another to an old American correspondent with
whom over the years he had exchanged many letters on
matters of folklore, myth, and similarly obscure anthropological subjects, a man his senior by a number of years,
the extremely erudite Wingate Peaslee, until recently
Professor of Psychology at Miskatonic University in
Massachusetts; and finally the third to an old charlatan of
a medium, known and endeared to him of old, one
Mother Quarry of Marshfield near Bristol.

The plot was this: without waiting for answers to the
letters, we would send the eggs first to Professor Peaslee
in America. Peaslee would of course receive his airmail

letter fractionally earlier than the air-parcel containing the eggs. Titus had more than enough faith in his friend to be satisfied that his instructions would be followed to the letter. Those instructions were simply to send the eggs on within twenty-four hours to Rossiter McDonald in Stornoway. Similarly McDonald was instructed to send them on without too great a delay to Mother Quarry, and from that 'talented' lady they would eventually come back to me. I say 'back to me', because I took the box with me, neatly parcelled and ready to be posted, when I left Blowne House. I was to be instrumental in forging the first link in the postal chain. I also posted the letters on my way home.

I had agreed completely with my knowledgeable friend that the eggs must be out of Blowne House that night – indeed I had insisted upon it – for they had been there long enough already, and Crow had obviously started to feel the strain of their presence. He had admitted to nervously starting at every slightest creak of the floorboards, and for the first time since moving into his singular and oddly-atmosphered bungalow dwelling he had started to jump at the groans of certain vociferous trees in his garden.

But knowing what he knew, and believing what he – no, what *we* – now believed, his nervousness was nothing if not natural. In fact, the presence of those eggs in his house above all else, quite apart from the fact that he had lately been grossly overworking, was responsible for the rapid deterioration of his general well-being since I last saw him. It would, I believed, not have taken very much more to start him on that same degenerative path taken by Sir Amery Wendy-Smith!

It may readily be understood why I hardly slept a wink that night, but lay in bed in my grey-stone house tossing and turning and chewing over in my mind the bulk of the new concept I had been asked to accept. In fact I *had* accepted it, but its details still needed thinking on, if only to clarify the overall picture and remove any remaining fuzz from its edges. Truth to tell, though, my mind did seem more than slightly foggy, as if I were suffering from some sort of hangover. But of course there was another, more immediate reason for my insomnia – the box with the lustrous spheres lay on a small table beside my bed!

Restlessly pummelling my pillow (which I found myself doing every half hour or so), I turned things over in my mind a dozen times, looking for loopholes and finding none – neither in Crow's immediate plot to stop the burrowers beneath from regaining possession of their eggs, nor in the premises of his incredible fears themselves – and yet I knew that there was something basically *wrong*! I knew it. The fault was there, submerged at the back of my mind, but would not rise to the surface.

If only this brain-fog would lift. My mood of crushing depression had vanished, true, but now I had this god-awful mental smog to wade through!

Of course, I did not know Crow's correspondents, his friends of old, personally; but he had tremendous faith in them, and especially in Peaslee. In his letter to the professor Crow had outlined his entire perception of the fantastic threat against Earth – hypothetically and yet strongly enough to hint of his personal involvement – and in my own opinion, putting myself in the position of a vastly intelligent man on receipt of such a letter, Crow had endangered his whole case. I had bluntly pointed out to him, after listening to a reading of the hastily scrawled letter, that Peaslee might see it as the ravings of a deranged mentality. As Crow himself had said: 'I'm damned if I know whom I might confide in . . .' But he had only chuckled at the suggestion, saying that he thought it unlikely, and that in any case, if only for past

friendship's sake, Peaslee would comply with his require-
ments regarding the box of eggs.

He had reckoned on a maximum period of three weeks
for the round trip of the eggs, but had taken the trouble
to request in addition confirmatory letters with regard to
their safe dispatch. I thought on this, and –

There it was again!

Now what *was* this twinge I kept getting at the back of
my mind whenever I thought of the journey the eggs
would commence in the morning?

But no, whenever I tried to nail the thing down it faded
away, back into the mists of my mind. I had known this
frustrating sensation before, and recognized the unsatis-
factory solution: simply to ignore it and let the thing
resolve itself in its own time. It was, nevertheless, annoying – and more than worrying in the circumstances.

Then, turning in my bed, my eyes would light on the
box with its enigmatic contents, and I could picture those
contents in my mind's eye, faintly luminous with that
pearly sheen of theirs in the darkness of their cardboard
coffin. That would set me off tangentially on yet another
mental tack.

I had asked Crow about that *other* box, the 'incubator',
discovered by Wendy-Smith at the site of dead G'harne.
Why, I had wanted to know, had there been no similar
receptacle in the tunnel-cave at Harden? But the tired
occultist (should I call him 'occultist' or 'scientist'?) had
been almost equally at a loss. He had finally hazarded,
after giving the matter some thought, that possibly conditions in that deep dark place had been more nearly perfect
for the incubation of the eggs than in the shallow hatchery
at G'harne.

But what of the *pictures* on that box, I had further
probed? – at which my learned friend had simply shuddered, saying that he might only direct me, as Sir Amery

had once directed his nephew, to the works of Commodus and the hag-ridden Caracalla. The pictures in his dreams had been more than enough without dwelling on the horrors others had known; for there had been more than simply blind, cephalopod obscenity to those nightmares of his. Likewise he believed that Bentham's cave-pictures had contained far more than the man had cared to mention – and perhaps understandably! This had whetted my curiosity all the more, so that I had pressed Crow until finally he had given in to me and described, all too clearly, some of those pictures of his dreams.

In some of them, he had told me, there had been an almost symbolic reaching towards the surface, a group-stretching of hideous tentacles; and in others, plainly surface scenes as opposed to subterrene – in those there had been sheer horror!

Vividly I remembered Crow's mode of *expression*, the cracked hollowness of his voice as he had said: 'There were four of them in one dream-fragment, de Marigny, rearing like caterpillars on their haunches, mouths agape – and they had a woman between them, pulling her to pieces and slobbering while the blood gushed and slopped . . .'

'But how,' I had morbidly demanded, my voice a whisper, 'could creatures without heads have . . . *mouths*?' Even asking my question I had known that I would not like the answer.

'Try thinking in less routine terms, Henri,' Crow had quietly advised. 'But whatever you do don't think on it too long, or with too great an attention to detail. They're so very – *alien* – these things.'

The memory of Crow's words and the way he had said them saw me reaching from my bed in one convulsive instant to switch on the light. I could not help it but a line from Ibn Schacabao's ancient and cryptic *Reflections* had sprung unbidden to my mind, a line I knew had been repeated by Alhazred in the *Necronomicon*: 'Evil the mind that is held by no head!' Ye gods! Minds and mouths without heads!

I am not normally a nervous man – God knows that if such were the case I should long ago have given up certain of my more *outré* interests – but with those eggs in their box beside my bed, and with the knowledge that somewhere, far away or perhaps not so far, deep down in the earth, monstrous burrowers *even now* burned and bubbled in the ground – well, who could say that merely illuminating my bedroom was an act of cowardice?

But in any case, even with the light on, I found myself no less apprehensive. There were shadows now where none had been before – thrown by my wardrobe, my dressing gown hanging on the door – so that before I knew it I found myself calculating how long it would take me to get out of bed and through the window in the event of –

I reached out again to switch off the light, purposely turning my back on the cardboard box in an attempt to put its contents from my mind . . .

Perhaps I did sleep then for a little while, for I remember a merging of my own drowsing thoughts with Crow's descriptions of some of his dreams as I recalled their telling; and when this brought me sweatingly back to wakefulness I also remembered his explanation of how he had first been alerted to the existence of the cthonian menace.

It had been those chants heard in his latter dreams of the burrowers; those chants containing the tell-tale name of a legendary city – G'harne! Remembering Wendy-Smith's expedition in search of that place, and something of the disastrous results, and then tying in certain of the newer contents of his voluminous cuttings-file and the details of his underground nightmares themselves, Crow had been led on to the Wendy-Smith document. That document, along with the letter of explanation obtained from Raymond Bentham, had clinched the thing in his mind. The remainder had been merely his normal follow-through of intelligently applied, if weirdly-inspired, logic.

We had also talked on the spread of Shudde-M'ell and his kin, and had given more thought to the horror's release from the prison of the Elder Gods. Crow was inclined to the belief that some natural cataclysm had freed the horror-deity, and I could see no better explanation, but *how long ago* had this convulsion of the Earth occurred – and how far had the cancer spread since then? Wendy-Smith had seemed concerned with the same problem, but Crow had seen Sir Amery's suggestions regarding a means of combating the creatures as ludicrous.

'Think of it, de Marigny, ' he had told me. 'Just *think* of trying to destroy the likes of Shudde-M'ell with flame-throwers! Why, these beings themselves are almost volcanic. They must be! Think of the temperatures and pressures required to fuse carbon and chrysolite and whatever else into the diamond-dust composition of those eggshells! And their ability to burn their way through solid rock. Flamethrowers? Hah! They'd delight in the very flames! It truly amazes me, though, the changes these beings must go through between infancy and adulthood. And yet, is it really so surprising? Human beings, I suppose, go through equally fantastic alterations – infancy, puberty, menopause, senility – and what about the amphibians, frogs, and toads . . . and the lepidopterous cycle? Yes, I can quite believe that Sir Amery killed off those two "babies" of his with a cigar – but by God it will take something more than that for an adult!'

And on the secret, subterranean spread of the horrors since that tremendous blunder of nature which he believed had freed them, Crow had likewise had his own ideas:

'Disasters, Henri! Look at the list of disasters caused by so-called "natural" seismic shocks, particularly in the last hundred years. Oh, I know we can't blame every tremor on Shudde-M'ell – if he, or *it*, still survives as godhead to its race – but, by heaven, we can certainly tag him with some of them! We already have the list put together by Paul Wendy-Smith; not big stuff, but costing lives nevertheless. Chinchon, Calahorra, Agen, Aisne, and so on. But what about Agadir? My God, but wasn't *that* a horror? And Agadir is not far off the route they took to England back in 1933. Look at the *size* of Africa, Henri. Why! In the other direction the things could have spread themselves all over that great continent by now – the entire Middle East even! It all depends on how many they were originally. And yet, there couldn't have been too many, despite Wendy-Smith's "hordes". No, I don't think that the Elder Gods would ever have allowed that. But who knows how many eggs have hatched since then, or how many others are still waiting to hatch in unsuspected depths of rock? The more I think of it, the more hideous the threat grows in my mind.'

Finally, before I had left him, Crow had tiredly scribbled for me a list of books he believed I should research. The *Necronomicon* of course headed the list, for the connection of that book with the Cthulhu Cycle of myth was legendary. My friend had recommended the expurgated manuscript translation (in a strictly limited edition for scholarly study only), by Henrietta Montague from the British Museum's black-letter. He had known Miss Montague personally, had been by her side when she died of some unknown wasting disease only a few weeks after completing her work on the *Necronomicon* for the Museum authorities. I knew that my friend blamed that work for her death; which was one of the reasons why he had warned me time and time again regarding too comprehensive a study of the book's contents. It was therefore understood that I should merely extract those sections directly concerning Shudde-M'ell and beings like him but keep, as far as possible, from becoming too involved with the book as a whole. Crow himself would arrange for a copy of Miss Montague's scholarly work to be put at my disposal.

Next on the list had been Ibn Schacabao's *Reflections*, also at the British Museum but under glass because of its short life expectancy. Although the museum had taken the usual precautions – chemical treatment had been applied, photostat copies made (one of which I would have to read, and more thoroughly than at that time some years previously) – still the venerable tome was gradually rotting away.

The list continued with two little known books by Commodus and Caracalla respectively, simply for the sake of their authors having been given mention by Wendy-Smith, and directly after these there followed the translated sections of the almost unfathomable *Pnakotic Manuscript* for the same reason. Similarly was Eliphas Lévi's *History of Magic* listed, and finally, this time from Crow's own shelves (he had carefully wrapped it for me), his copy of the infamous *Cultes des Goules*. He had scanned the latter book so often himself that he was fearful of missing something important in a further personal perusal. On my inquiring, he told me he did, however, intend to give special personal attention to the *Cthaat Aquadingen*; there was much in that hideously bound book – particularly in the two middle chapters, which Crow long ago had had separately bound – that might very well apply. Most of these writings, as I have previously stated, I had read before, but without a definite purpose other than occult and macabre curiosity.

It could, I suppose, be reasoned that my itinerary should also include the *G'harne Fragments*, and of course it would have, if that mass of crumbling, centuried shards had been in any one of the four languages with which I am familiar! As it was, there had been only two supposed authorities on the fragments: Sir Amery Wendy-Smith, who left nothing of his decipherings behind, and Professor Gordon Walmsley of Goole, whose 'spoof notes' contained what purported to be whole chapters of translations from the *G'harne Fragments*' cryptic ciphers, but which had been mocked as absurd fakery by any number of reliable authorities. For these reasons Crow had omitted the fragments from his list.

All these and other thoughts flew around in my strangely misty mind, until eventually I must have drowsed off again.

My next remembered thought was that of hearing, seemingly close at hand, the dreadful droning and buzzing of monstrously alien voices – but it was not until I found myself awake and leaping from my bed on wildly trembling legs, my hair standing up straight on my head, that I realized I had only been dreaming. The sun was already up, filling the day outside with light.

And yet even then there echoed in my ears those loathsome, monotonously buzzing tones of horror. And they were in my mind exactly as they had been in Wendy-Smith's document:

> Ce'haiie ep-ngh fl'hur G'harne fhtagn,
> Ce'haiie fhtagn ngh Shudde-M'ell.
> Hai G'harne orr'e ep fl'hur,
> Shudde-M'ell ican-icanicas fl'hur orr'e G'harne.

As the thing finally faded away and disappeared, I shook my head and numbly moved back over to my bedside table to pick up the cardboard box and feel its weight. I examined the box minutely, still more than half asleep. I honestly do not know what I expected to find, but I found nothing. All was as it had been the night before.

I washed, shaved, and dressed, and had hardly returned from mailing the parcel of eggs to Professor Peaslee from a local post office – all done very lethargically – when the telephone rang. It was quite insistent, clamouring like mad, but for some reason I hesitated before picking it up to put the receiver timorously to my ear.

'De Marigny? It's Crow here.' My friend's voice was urgent, electrical. 'Listen. Have you sent off the eggs yet?'

'Why, yes – I just managed to catch the morning post.'

'Oh, no!' he groaned; then: 'Henri, do you still have that houseboat at Henley?'

'Why, yes. In fact, it's been in use until recently. Some friends of mine. I told them they could have it for a week just before I went to France. They're off the boat now, though; I got the key back in a little parcel in last night's mail. But why?' Despite my question I felt oddly listless, growing more disinterested by the second.

'Pack yourself some things, Henri, enough to live with decently for a fortnight or so. I'll pick you up within the hour in the Mercedes. I'm just loading my stuff now.'

'Eh?' I asked, completely uncomprehending, not really wanting to know. 'Stuff?' The mists were thick in my mind. 'Titus' – I heard myself as if from a hundred miles away – 'what's wrong?'

'Everything is *wrong*, Henri, and in particular my reasoning! Haven't you heard the morning news or read the newspapers?'

'No,' I answered through a wall of thickening fog. 'I'm just up. Slept badly.'

'Bentham is dead, de Marigny! The poor devil – a "subsidence" at Alston. We're going to have to drastically revise our thinking. The houseboat is a godsend.'

'Eh? What?'

'The houseboat, Henri! It's a godsend! Like Sir Amery said: "They don't like water." I'll see you within the hour.'

'Titus,' I gropingly answered, barely managing to catch him before he could break the connection, 'not today, for God's sake! I . . . I really don't feel up to it. I mean . . . it's a damned nuisance – '

'Henri, I – ' He faltered, amazement in his voice; then, in a tone full of some strange understanding: 'So, they've been at you, have they?' Now he was deliberate and calm. 'Well, not to worry. Be seeing you.' And with that the line went dead.

I don't know how much later it was when the infernal banging came at my door, and the ringing at my doorbell, but for quite a long time I simply ignored it. Then, despite an urge to close my eyes and go back to sleep where I sat in my chair, I managed to get up and go to the door. Yawningly I opened it – and was almost bowled over as a frenzied figure in black rushed in.

It was of course Titus Crow – but his eyes were blazing in a strange and savage passion completely alien to his character as I had previously known it!

6

That is Not Dead

(From de Marigny's Notebooks)

'De Marigny!' Crow exploded as soon as he was inside and had the door shut behind him. 'Henri, you've been got at!'

'Eh? Got at?' I sleepily replied. 'No such thing, Titus – I'm tired, that's all.' Yet despite my odd lethargy I was still slightly curious. 'How do you mean, "Got at"? By whom?'

Quickly taking my arm and leading me, half dragging me to my own study, he answered: 'Why, the burrowers beneath, of course! Your place isn't protected as Blowne House is. I might have expected as much. To leave you with those things all night. Even my place hasn't got full protection – far from it.'

'Protection?' My brief interest was already on the wane, so that when I flopped down again in my easy chair I was hardly bothered whether he answered me or not. 'Really, you do make a fuss, old man!' (I had never before in my life called Titus Crow 'old man'; I probably never will again.) I felt my eyes closing, listening to my own voice almost abstractedly as it rambled slowly, falteringly on:

'Look. I've had a bad night, got up too early. I'm very tired – very tired . . .'

'Yes, that's right, you have yourself a nap, Henri,' he told me in a soothing voice. 'I can manage what needs to be done on my own.'

'Manage?' I mumbled. 'Something needs to be done?'

Peering through half closed lids I saw that Crow had already started – but what was he doing? His eyes were wide, blazing fanatically as he stood in the centre of my room with his arms and hands held open and up in a typically sorcerous stance. This time, however, Titus Crow was not conjuring anything, but rather *putting something down* – or at least, holding something back, if only temporarily.

I have since recognized the alien syllables he used then, in Feery's *Notes on the Necronomicon* (I still have not read any other copy of the work, in any form), where they appear as follows:

> Ya na kadishtu nilgh'ri stell'bsna Nyogtha,
> K'yarnak phlegethor l'ebumna syha'h n'ghft,
> Ya hai kadishtu ep r'luh-eeh Nyogtha eeh,
> S'uhn-ngh athg li'hee orr'e syha'h.

When he had done with the Vach-Viraj Incantation, for his fantastic utterances had consisted of nothing less, Crow proceeded to take from his pocket a small vial of clear liquid which he sparingly splashed about the room. Still splashing, he went out into the other rooms to continue this cryptic occupation until my entire house had been cleansed; I knew, of course, that my friend's activities were exorcismal.

Nor were his thaumaturgies pointless or to no effect, for, already feeling more my old self, I knew that Crow had been right – I *had* been under the influence of Shudde-M'ell, his brothers or minions.

As soon as he reentered my study Crow saw that I was back to normal and grinned in a self-satisfied if nervous manner. By that time, shaken though I naturally was, I was already packing books and papers into a large case. My mazed mind, as if vacuum-cleaned, had been emptied of all enfeebling thoughts and ideas by my friend's 'White Magic'; or rather, by the 'Science' of the Elder Gods!

It took me only the matter of a further half hour or so to complete my packing (I made certain to include a favourite fetish of mine, a rather old and ornate pistol, once the property of the witch-hunting Baron Kant), lock the house up, and accompany Titus out to his Mercedes with my cases. Moments later we were on our way.

We made three stops on our way out to Henley, the first of which was to allow us to get off hurried telegrams to Mother Quarry, McDonald, and Professor Peaslee, warning them in no uncertain manner to send off the parcel of eggs *as soon as it arrived* without first opening it, and hinting strongly of grave dangers should they delay even in the slightest. This of course had been made necessary by the death of Bentham; an explanation may be in order and I will give it later. The second stop was for lunch at Beaconsfield, where we found a friendly pub and sat out in a small sunny garden to enjoy cold beer with chicken sandwiches. The third call was at an adequate library in Marlow, where Crow was obliged to become a member in order to borrow a number of anthropological works supplementary to those we already had with us.

By 3:30 P.M. we were aboard *Seafree*, my four-berth houseboat, and getting ourselves settled in. Where I had her moored, at a spot some distance out of Henley itself, the Thames is quite deep and Crow seemed satisfied that we were safe there for the moment from any physical manifestations of the burrowers. After we had made the place immediately livable and packed our stuff away, we were able to sit down and talk seriously of the fresh developments. The drive down to Henley, apart from our stops, had in the main been quiet; Crow dislikes being distracted while driving, and I had had time to sort out fresh points to raise and questions to ask during the journey.

Now I could learn the hows and whys of my friend's earlier obscure exorcismal activities on my behalf at my house. Crow told me of the Black-Letter Text *Necronomicon* – notably the Kester Library copy in Salem, Massachusetts – which contains the following passage, incomplete in Feery's notes but known to Titus Crow of old:

Men know him as the Dweller in Darkness, that brother of the Old Ones called Nyogha, the Thing that should not be. He can be summoned to Earth's surface through certain secret caverns and fissures, and sorcerers have seen him in Syria and below the Black Tower of Leng; from the Thang Grotto of Tartary he has come ravening to bring terror and destruction among the pavilions of the great Khan. Only by the Looped Cross, by the Vach-Viraj Incantation and by the Tikkoun Elixir may he be driven back to the nighted caverns of hidden foulness where he dwelleth.

Thus, as a protection against this Nyogtha, I could well understand the use of the Vach-Viraj Incantation – but against the burrowers . . .? Crow explained that he had used the chant at my house because he believed *all* the Cthulhu Cycle Earth deities to be related, either physically or mentally, and that any charm having definite power against any one of them must be capable of at least *some* influence over the others. Indeed, the immediate effect of his – occult? – remedies had been to clear my place (not to mention my mind) of the influences exerted through dreams of Shudde-M'ell or his deputies; which was more really than Crow had expected. However, he also explained that he believed the chant and elixir to have no lasting strength, except against Nyogtha – who or whatever he may be! – but he has never explained to me just what further 'protections' there are about Blowne House. I suspect, though, that these are far superior to any signs, sigils, runes, or cantrips of which I am ever likely to become aware.

* * *

The next four days passed quickly at Henley, and were taken up mainly in making *Seafree* more livable and in long think-tank sessions between Crow and myself on our various problems. Had I not been around at that time to supply the obvious words of exoneration, I believe Crow might well have started to blame himself for Bentham's death. I pointed out that knowing as little of the burrowers as we knew, which had been even less at the time Crow last wrote to the Northerner, his advice to Bentham in the matter had been expert. In fact, looking back on it, I was now surprised at the amount of time it had taken the Cthonians (the name Crow eventually settled on for the subterranean spawn) to seek Bentham out and deal with him! Harden is not all that far from Alston. Crow had insisted, however, that there had been a direct parallel – one which he had missed in what, according to him, had been tantamount to criminal neglect.

He referred of course to Paul Wendy-Smith's disappearance – that vanishment which we now knew must be laid at the door, or burrow, of the Cthonians – following that of his uncle, and which had occurred *after* the discovery of their cigar-murdered infants by the Cthonians. It was all too apparent now that one did not need to be in actual possession of those crystal spheres to attract adults of the species. Having *been* in possession – even in close contact – seemed reason enough to provoke hideous retaliation; which explained, naturally, Crow's haste in getting himself out of Blowne House and both of us out of London in the first place! Too (I had realized immediately), this had been the elusive something flickering at the back of my mind that night before the Cthonians first 'invaded' me; by token of which I knew that, if blame existed at all, I must hold myself equally to blame alongside Crow. The simple fact that Paul Wendy-Smith had never actually possessed the eggs, but the Cthonians had nevertheless taken him, should have made itself apparent to both of us sooner.

And yet, even in my houseboat on the Thames, which Crow had at first proclaimed safe, over the last few days my erudite friend had grown ever the more nervous and far from happy regarding our continued well-being. The Cthonians could still find us, or so he seemed to believe, through dreams. In this, as in so many things, Crow proved to be absolutely correct.

Because of the possibility of our eventual discovery, we had early decided that our first task would be to see if we could find any *positive* counterspells (Crow referred to them as 'devices' – I preferred to think in the old 'magic' terms) against an attack. We could not, after all, remain on the houseboat indefinitely; in fact we had already taken to relaxing for an hour or so each evening in the bar of a pub not one hundred yards away down the river bank, well within sprinting distance of *Seafree*! In the furtherance of this project I had given over most of my time to correlating all the written knowledge at my disposal on the pentacle, the five-pointed Star of Power, whose design had been originated by the Great Elder Gods in the construction of their evil-imprisoning star-stones.

Now, to my mind it is not surprising that much is made of the pentacle or pentagram in so-called 'cabalistic' works – the paperback junk which clutters so many modern bookstalls, supposedly culled from the great forbidden books – but quite apart from such references I found many disturbing tangential allusions in fairly contemporary verse, in literature, even in art. Admittedly, such works as contained these oblique or obscure references were generally by persons deeply attracted to things mysterious or macabre – mystics, mages, and usually (broadly speaking) persons gifted with rare imaginations and paradoxically *outré* insight – but nevertheless the 'pentacle theme' seemed, at one time or another, to have captured the imaginations of an inordinately large number of these artistic people.

Gerhardt Schrach, the Westphalian philosopher, has said: 'It fascinates me . . . that such a perfect figure can be drawn with only five straight lines . . . five triangles, joined at their bases, where they form a pentagon . . . perfectly pentameral . . . *powerful* . . . and fascinating!' It was Schrach, too, in his *Thinkers Ancient and Modern*, who pointed out for me the Hittite practice of spreading the fingers of one hand before the face of an enemy or evil person and saying: 'The Star upon thee, Dark One!' – which was recognized as a certain protection against the evil intentions of any person so confronted.

Other than Schrach and many other contemporary writers and philosophers, there were also a number of painters whose works, I knew, had from time to time featured the star motif: noticeably Chandler Davies in many of his designs for *Grotesque* before that magazine folded; particularly his full-page black and white 'Stars and Faces', so strangely disturbing and horrific that it was now in itself a valuable collector's item. William Blake too, the painter, poet, and mystic, had not neglected the theme, and had used it strikingly in his 'Portrait of a Flea' – in which the central horror is actually *prisoned by five-pointed stars!* And while I knew the point could be argued, still, remembering Blake's stars, I found them disturbingly akin to my own mental picture of the star-stones of ancient Mnar.

On the other hand, in Edmund Pickman Derby's book of nightmare lyrics, *Azathoth and Other Horrors*, there was one clearly blatant reference to the five-pointed star as a weapon against 'Greater Gods by far', whatever gods he alluded to; and such were the other many references to be discovered that I soon found myself interested in my task almost beyond the present requirement.

It was on the fourth night, while I was making notes of this sort and trying to find in them some sort of order or clue, that Titus dozed off. He had been working hard all that day – not physical work but intense mental concentration – and had actually fallen asleep over his copy of the *Cthaat Aquadingen*. I noticed the fact and smiled. It was good that he should get some rest: I was already fatigued myself, both physically and mentally, and Crow had been familiar with the problem far longer than I.

Shortly before midnight I too must have dozed off, for the first thing I knew was that someone was shouting.

It was Crow.

I came awake immediately from monstrous dreams (mercifully unremembered considering what was soon to come), to find my friend still asleep but locked in the throes of nightmare.

He was sitting in his chair, his head forward on his folded arms where they rested on the open *Cthaat Aquadingen* atop the small table at which he had been working. His whole body was jerking and twitching spasmodically and he was shouting snatches of incomprehensible occult jargon. I hastened from my chair to waken him.

'Eh? What?' he gasped as I shook him. 'Look out, de Marigny – *they're here!*' He jumped to his feet, shaking visibly, cold sweat glistening upon his face. 'They . . . they're . . . here?'

He sat down again, still trembling, and poured himself a glass of brandy. 'My God! What a nightmare, Henri! They've managed to get through to me this time, all right – picked my brains clean, I imagine. They'll know where we are now, for sure.'

'The Cthonians? It was . . . them?' I breathlessly asked.

'Oh, yes! Definitely. And they made no pretext, didn't bother to hide their identity. I had the impression they were trying to tell me something – attempting to, well, *bargain* with me. Hah! That would be like making a pact with all the devils of hell! And yet there were tones of desperation, too, in the messages I received. Damned if I know what *they* could be frightened of. I simply had the feeling that we're not alone in all this, that reinforcements are being rushed up to the front, as it were! Damned peculiar.'

'I don't follow you, Titus,' I said, shaking my head. 'You're being a bit vague, you know.'

'Then I'd best tell you all my dream contained, Henri, and then we'll see what you make of it,' he replied.

'First off, there were no pictures, no visual hallucinations – which, it could be argued, are what dreams are really made of – but merely . . . *impressions!* I was floating in a greyness, the colourless substance of the subconscious psyche, if you like, and these . . . *impressions* . . . kept coming to me. I knew it was the Cthonians – their thoughts, their mental sendings, are so very alien – but I couldn't shut them out of my mind. They were telling me to stop interfering, to let sleeping dogs lie. What do you make of that?'

Before I could answer, even if I had an answer, he hurriedly continued:

'Then I got these fear-impressions I mentioned, a nameless dread of some obscure, ill-defined possibility with which I was somehow involved. I don't know for sure, but I don't think it was intended that I should read these fear-impressions. I'm a fraction more psychic than these horrors are used to, I suspect – a fact well in our favour. But overall it was, I don't know, as if they were trying to *bribe* me! "Get out while you can, Titus Crow, and we'll leave you alone," sort of thing. "You don't have our eggs any more and so we're willing to lose interest in you – provided you'll leave us alone and not go meddling where you're not wanted!"'

'Then we're on the right track, Titus,' I broke in. 'We've got them worried!'

He looked at me, more under control now, and slowly grinned. 'It certainly seems so, de Marigny, but I wish to God I knew what it is they're so worried about! Still, as you say, we must be on the right track. It's good to know that, at least. I'd love to know, though, where Peaslee and the others fit in – '

'What's that, Titus?' I asked. Again he had lost me.

'I'm sorry, Henri, of course you can't follow me,' he quickly apologized. 'You see, there were in these impressions *references* – don't ask me to clarify – to Peaslee and certain others; like Bernard Jordan, the skipper of one of those seagoing drilling-rigs I was telling you about. He was a very lucky man, according to my cuttings. The lone survivor when his rig, *Sea-Maid*, went to the bottom off Hunterby Head. And there was mention of someone else, someone I've never even heard of before. Hmm,' he mused, frowning. 'Now who on earth is David Winters? Anyway, I had the feeling that the Cthonians were far more afraid of these other chaps than they could ever be of me! I was warned, in effect, to keep away from these other people. Rather astonishing, really. After all, I've never met Professor Peaslee in the flesh, and I couldn't even guess at where to begin looking for this Jordan chap. And as for David Winters, well . . .'

'You were screaming, Titus,' I told him, holding his shoulder. 'You were shouting something or other which I couldn't quite make out. Now what was all that about?'

'Ah! That would have been my denial, Henri. Of course, I refused their ultimatum. I tried to throw spells at them, particularly the Vach-Viraj Incantation, to get them out of my mind. But it didn't work. En masse, their minds were too strong for such simple devices. They overcame them easily.'

'Ultimatum?' I questioned. 'There were . . . threats?'

'Yes, and horrible threats,' he grimly answered. 'They told me – that they would "show me their powers", in some sort of way or other, which was when you woke me up. Anyway, they're not rid of me yet, not by a long shot, but we may have to move on from here. Three or four more days is about as much time as we can afford to stay, I should think, before moving on.'

'Yes,' I answered. 'Well, frankly, I couldn't move tonight at gunpoint. I'm dead on my feet. Let's get some sleep, if they'll let us, and make fresh plans tomorrow.'

For myself, I did get to sleep all right – I *was* quite 'dead on my feet' – but I can't speak for Titus Crow. I know that I seemed in my slumbers to hear his voice, low and muttering, and that it seemed a very long time before the echoes of the Vach-Viraj Incantation and certain other runes of elder spheres faded in the caves of my subconscious.

Strangely, by noon the next day we were better settled in our minds, as if the knowledge that the Cthonians had found something to fear in us had lifted momentarily the bleak veil of strange dread, nervous tension and mental fatigue that had been hanging over us.

It had not been difficult to reason out just why it had taken Shudde-M'ell's nightmare brothers so long to discover our hideaway. Up until the previous night, Crow had been using the Vach-Viraj Incantation and the Tikkoun Elixir nightly, when, at last, he had run out of the latter. Evidently the liquid which compounded that strange and potent brew (I was later to learn just what it was) had had much to do with keeping the Cthonian dream-sendings and -searchings at bay, Plainly, this late deficiency in our defences had been sufficient to allow them to find our subconscious minds and thus discover our location.

Later it was to become plain why the knowledge that our whereabouts was known to the Cthonians did not panic us; why Crow's dream, rather than startling us into headlong flight, had served instead – after the initial shock – to calm us down.

As it was, we reasoned that if the burrowers did indeed intend to make an attack, well, they still had the water of the river to combat, and in any case they were unlikely to attempt anything in the daylight hours. The obvious trick, if the Cthonians could manage it, would be to lure us from *Seafree* of an evening after dark, an eventuality against which we made precautionary plans. At last light each evening, until we left the houseboat for good, we would simply lock the cabin-cum-sleeper door (equipped with a stout padlock on the inside), and, since I seemed more susceptible to the dream-sendings of the Cthonians, Crow would keep the key. It now seems amazing to me that once again we both failed to see a parallel which, obvious as it should have been, proved us both totally at fault in our reasoning; simply that Paul Wendy-Smith had been taken *in daylight*, or dusk at the very latest! However, our plan, faulty as it was, meant that we would have to deny ourselves the occasional evening trip to the Old Mill Inn.

Now, I don't want to give the impression that we two were alcoholics – though we might have had very good reasons to become such – but Crow did like his brandy of a night, and I am not averse to a noggin myself. We had already stocked up with provisions for a fortnight, and so decided we had best do the same regarding liquid refreshments. With this in mind we decided on lunch at the Old Mill Inn, when we would also purchase a bottle or two.

Our timing was perfect, for we had no sooner seated ourselves in the smoke-room when the ex-Guardsman proprietor came over to our table. We had of course met him before, but on this occasion he introduced himself properly and Crow reciprocated on our behalf.

'Ah! So you *are* Mr Crow! Well, that saves me a walk down to the houseboat.'

'Oh?' Crow's interest picked up. 'Did you want to see me, then? Do sit down, Mr Selby. Will you join us in a drink?'

The huge proprietor thanked us, went over to the bar and poured himself a half-pint from a bottle, then returned with his glass and sat down. 'Yes,' he began, 'I had a telephone call for you this morning – very garbled and hard to understand – from someone who was checking on your being here. Told me you'd be using the houseboat *Seafree*. I said I wasn't sure of your names, but that there were two gentlemen on the houseboat.'

'Did he say who he was?' Puzzled as to who might know of our whereabouts, I got the question in before Crow. I could see that my friend was equally at a loss.

'Yes, sir,' he answered me. 'I wrote his name down on a scrap of paper. Here we are.' He dug into his waistcoat pocket. 'Said he'd drop in on you this evening – if you were still here. The conversation was a bit confused, but I gathered he was calling from a booth somewhere nearby. Anything wrong, sir?'

Titus had taken the slip of paper and read it. His already tired face, at a stroke, had gone deathly white. His hands shook violently as he passed me the slip. I took it from him and smoothed it down on the tabletop.

I took a sip at my drink – *and then choked on it as the meaning of what was scrawled on the paper finally drove home!*

It was, as Selby had said, simply a name:
Amery Wendy-Smith!

7

Not from His Charnel Clay

(From de Marigny's Notebooks)

All afternoon and until 10:30 that night – earlier on deck, later in the light of a paraffin-lamp in the cabin – Crow and I talked in awed whispers on the fantastic vistas opened by the totally unpredictable 'message' we had received at the inn.

It made no difference that all day long the sun had blazed roastingly down on the river from the glorious June sky, or that small river-craft had been purring upstream and down by the dozen while lovers walked on the green banks and waved to us at our mooring. For us the physical warmth of the sun had been chilled by the fearful knowledge of that horror which lurked deep beneath England's unique green; and though the songs of the birds and the laughter of the couples had been loud enough, we had talked, as I have said, in hushed whispers.

For Crow had made no bones of his firm belief that Sir Amery was indeed dead, and that therefore this latest . . . *manifestation* . . . was nothing less than another gambit of the Cthonians. Had there been a third player in our game – that is, someone who like Crow and myself knew of the dreadful activities of the burrowers beneath – then we *might* have been able to lay the blame for this latest shock at that person's feet; but there was no one. In any case, the telephone call would have been a pretty gruesome leg-pull.

And of course Crow was absolutely right in his assertion. He had to be. The unknown caller could not possibly be Sir Amery Wendy-Smith; I knew that as soon as I was able to give the matter a little reasonable thought. Why,

Sir Amery had been anything but a young man back in 1937. Now? He would be well on his way towards his centenary! Few men live so long, and fewer still manage to *live and hide themselves away*, for no apparent reason, for over a third of their century!

No, I was as sure as Titus Crow that this was simply another ruse of the Cthonians. How they had pulled it off was another matter. Crow had pondered the possibility (very briefly), that his closest neighbour, an ecclesiastical doctor who lived a hundred yards or so from Blowne House, might have been responsible for the stunning 'message'; for apparently he had given the good reverend our forwarding address prior to leaving Blowne House. He had also asked this same gentleman to accept transferred telephone calls for him, which had been agreed, but had warned him to divulge our whereabouts only to bona fida persons. It seemed that the doctor had assisted him on a number of ticklish occasions before. But this time not even that worthy had known of Crow's reason for rushing off to Henley, and he had probably never even heard of Sir Amery Wendy-Smith. In fact, *no one* knew of our reason for being at Henley – except, since last night, the Cthonians themselves!

And yet, what could the burrowers possibly hope to gain from so transparent a ploy? This was a question I had put to my friend, to which he had answered:

'Well, Henri, I think we'd better ask "how" before we ask "why" – I like to see the whole picture whenever it's possible. I've been giving it some thought, though, and it seems to me that our phantom telephone caller must be a person "under the influence" of the Cthonians. I imagine they must have such – assistants, a point we'd best look out for in the future. We've been thinking in terms of horror and hideous death at the hands – the tentacles – of monstrous subterranean beings, but we can just as easily

105

die from gunshot wounds! Now then, taking all that into account, we can ask ourselves why did the Cthonians use so transparent a ploy, as you had it, and I believe I know the answer.'

For once I foresaw his conclusion: 'I think I see what you're getting at.'

'Oh?'

'Yes. We've both stated over the last few days that we think we're pretty safe here on the houseboat, though you have had your doubts. Now, just suppose that *They* think so too; that *They* can't touch us physically while we're here. Why, the obvious solution would be to get us out of here, scare us into abandoning the boat and taking to dry land!'

'Right,' he answered. 'And this impossible telephone call serves as a second persuasion, to follow up the warning dream the Cthonians sent me last night. Go on, de Marigny.'

'Well, that's it!' I cried. 'That's all there is to it. Following your dream, this message – which we know must have its origin with the Cthonians – was simply to give their warning substance; to let us know that we're far from safe here, and that our best bet is to – '

'To get the hell out of it?'

'Yes.'

'So what do you suggest?'

'That we stay *right where we are!*'

'Yes,' he answered, 'and that's exactly what we're going to do! It begins to look more and more to me as though we're as safe here as we can be. As you say, this makes the second Cthonian attempt to get us away from the river – which is, I agree, a damn good reason for us to stay put! So, for the time being at least, we'll stay. We have at least two weapons against them: the river and the Vach-Viraj Incantation.' He frowned thoughtfully. 'We should have more of the Tikkoun Elixir shortly, by the way, if the Reverend Harry Townley keeps his promise. Townley's the neighbour I told you about. He said he'd send me on a supply; and he's never let me down before.'

'The Reverend Townley?' I frowned. 'The Tikkoun Elixir . . . ?'

The answer slotted itself neatly into place in my mind. 'You mean that the elixir is – '

'Yes, of course,' he answered, nodding his head, surprise showing on his face. 'Hadn't I mentioned it before? He tossed me the empty vial, the contents of which had been used so well. 'Oh, yes! Holy Water, what else? We know already of Shudde-M'ell's hatred of water, so naturally water which carries in addition a blessing – well, it's potent against many a horror besides the Cthonians, believe me!'

'And how about the Looped Cross?' I asked, remembering the three forces potent against Nyoghtha as delineated in the *Necronomicon*. 'Does the Crux Ansata indeed have similar powers?'

'I believe so, yes, to a degree. I had meant to mention it to you earlier, last night when you were working on the star-stone theme. What do you have, Henri, if you break the loop at the top of the Crux Ansata?'

I pictured the image his words conjured in my mind – then snapped my fingers. 'Why! A symbol with *five* extremities, a crude representation of the Elder Sign, the prisoning star of the Cthulhu Cycle of myth!'

'Indeed, and the looped Tau Cross in Olden Khem was also a symbol of power – and a great symbol of generation! It was the *Ankh*, Henri! The very word means "soul" or "life" – a protection of life and soul. Oh, yes, I should certainly believe that the Crux Ansata has power.' He grinned wanly. 'I rather think, though, from your question, that your powers of observation can't be all that they used to be.'

'Eh? How do you mean?' I asked suspiciously, a trifle daunted.

'Why, if you look, you'll see!' he replied. 'On our first day here I nailed a tiny silver Crux Ansata to the door!'

For a moment, despite our situation and the seriousness of our conversation, I believed Crow was having me on. I had noticed no such thing. I got up quickly and crossed to the cabin door, opening it to peer at its contours in the glow of the deck- and cabin-lights. Sure enough, Crow's Looped Cross was there, at the very top of the door.

I had just turned back into the cabin, an exclamation of admiration on my lips, when the smell hit me. I say 'hit' me, and in all truth the cliché is quite void of exaggeration, for a positively vile *stench* was issuing from somewhere behind me on the midnight-black bank of the river.

There came footfalls . . .

Crow must have smelled it, too, and perhaps he heard the soft sounds from the quiet river bank. I saw him out of the corner of my eye as he jerked to his feet, his face pale in the flaring light, and then I concentrated on the darkness outside. I crouched there in the door, peering with bulging, fearful eyes into the shadows beyond the railed gangway.

Something moved there, a shape; and a low, clotted cough sounded – which was followed by a guttural, barely human voice!

'Ah, I see you're not . . . *glug* . . . expecting me, my friend! Didn't you get my message, then?'

I fell back as this reeking, awfully shadowed figure swayed up the gangplank. 'Please turn down the light, sir,' the clotted voice continued, 'and for God's sake . . . *glug* . . . have no fear of me. All will be explained.'

'Who – ?' I gulped, my voice barely audible. 'What – ?'

'Sir Amery Wendy-Smith – or at least his mind – at your service, sir. And would you be Titus Crow, or are you . . . *glug* . . . Henri-Laurent de Marigny?'

I fell back even more as the man-shaped, stinking black shadow stepped slowly closer; and then Crow's arm swept me aside and back into the cabin as he took my place at the door. In his hand he held my pistol, which had once belonged to Baron Kant.

'Stop right there!' he called out harshly, brokenly, to the black figure, now more than halfway up the gang-plank. 'You can't be Wendy-Smith – he's dead!'

'My body, sir – the body I used to have – is dead, yes . . . *glug* . . . but my mind lives on; at least for a little while longer! I sense that you are Titus Crow. Now, please turn down the deck-light . . . *glug* . . . and the lamp in the cabin, and let me talk to you.'

'This gun,' Crow countered, his voice shaking, 'fires silver bullets. I don't know what you are, but I believe I can destroy you!'

'My dear . . . *glug* . . . sir, I have *prayed* for destruction!' The figure took another lurching step forward. 'But before you . . . *glug* . . . attempt to grant me any such merciful release, at least let me tell you what I was sent to tell – let me deliver *Their* warning! And in any case, neither your gun, nor the Crux Ansata there on the door, not even your elixirs or . . . *glug* . . . chants can immobilize this body. It is the stuff of which Cthulhu himself is made, or very close to it! Now . . .' The clotted, almost slopping voice grew more articulate, speeding up in some sort of hideous hysteria: 'For God's sake, will you let me deliver the message I was sent to deliver?'

'Crow,' I nervously blurted, my hand trembling on his shoulder, 'what is it? *What in hell is it?*'

Instead of answering me, he leaned out of the door to

109

turn down the wick of the lamp we had hung near the head of the gangplank. He left the very smallest flame glowing there in the dark. The shadow became an inky namelessness swaying almost rhythmically on the gangplank.

'Titus!' I gasped, almost rigid with dread. 'By all that's holy – are you trying to get us killed?'

'Not a bit of it, Henri,' he whispered, his shaky voice belying its message, 'but I want to hear what this – *thing* – has to say. Do as you're bid. Turn down the lamp!'

'*What?*' I backed away from his figure framed in the doorway, almost willing to believe that the strain of the last few days had been too much for him.

'Please!' the guttural voice of the vile-smelling thing on the gangplank came again as its owner took another lurching step forward. 'Please, there is little enough time as it is. They won't let . . . *glug* . . . this body hold together much longer!'

At that Crow turned, thrusting me aside and hurrying to the paraffin-lamp to dim its hissing glare. This done, he placed a chair near the door and stepped back as the stars in the night sky were blotted out by the bulk of the nameless speaker when it appeared in the doorway. Stumblingly it half sat, half fell into the chair. There was a quite audible squelching sound as its contours moulded to the wooden frame.

By this time I had backed up to the bunks. Crow had perched himself on the small desk, feet firmly on the floor. He looked very brave in the dim, flickering light, but I preferred to believe he sat there because his legs were no longer capable of holding him up! Not a bad idea. I sat down abruptly on a lower bunk.

'Here,' my friend whispered, 'you'd better have this if you're so nervous. But don't use it – not unless you have to!' He tossed Kant's pistol over to me.

110

'Please listen.' The nodding blackness on the chair spoke again, its stench wafting all about the cabin in thick gusts, blown by the warm breeze from the open door. 'I have been sent by Them, by the horrors beneath, to deliver a message . . . *glug* . . . and to let you see what hell is like! They have sent me to – '

'Do you mean Shudde-M'ell?' Crow cut in, his voice a trifle stronger.

'Indeed.' The horror nodded. 'At least, by his brothers, his children.'

'What are you?' I found myself asking, hypnotized. 'You're not a . . . man!'

'I *was* a man.' The shape in the chair seemed to sob, its lumpy outline moving in the flickering shadows. 'I *was* Sir Amery Wendy-Smith. Now I am only his mind, his brain. But you must *listen*! It is only Their power that holds me together – and even They . . . *glug* . . . cannot keep this shape solid much longer!'

'Go on,' Crow said quietly, and I was astonished to discover a strange – compassion? – in his voice.

'This, then, is Their message. I am Their messenger and I bear witness to the truth of what They have to say. It is this: If you leave well enough alone, as of now, They will let you go in peace. They will bother you no more, neither in dreams nor in your waking moments. They will lift all . . . enchantments . . . *glug* . . . from your minds. If you persist – then in the end They will take you, and will do with you what They have done with me!'

'And what was that?' I asked in awed tones, still trembling violently, peering at the horror in the chair.

For while the voice of – Wendy-Smith? – had been speaking, I had allowed myself the luxury of simultaneous concentration, taking in all that was said but thinking equally clearly on other matters, and now I found myself straining to see the thing in the chair more clearly.

It looked as though our visitor was clad in a large black overcoat, turned up about his neck, and it looked, too, as if he must have something covering his head – which perhaps accounted for the clotted, distorted quality of his voice – for I had caught not a glimpse of any whiteness to suggest a face there atop the oddly lumpy body. My mind, I discovered, allowed freely to ponder other things, had trembled on the verge of a mental chasm; the mad observations of Abdul Alhazred in his *Necronomicon* as reported by Joachim Feery: '. . . Till out of corruption horrid life springs, and the dull scavengers of Earth wax crafty to vex it and swell monstrous to plague it . . .'

I hastily brought my wandering mind back under control.

The thing in the chair – which had allegedly been a man – was answering my question, telling what it was that the Cthonians had done to him, what they would do to Crow and me if we refused to do as they ordered.

'They . . . *glug* . . .' the clotted voice gobbled, 'They destroyed my body – *but kept my brain alive!* They housed my mind in a living envelope of Their manufacture; a shapeless, immobile mass of filth; but with veins and . . . *glug* . . . capillaries, and a heart of sorts – with all the machinery needed to keep a human mind alive! Don't ask me how They . . . *glug-glug* . . . did it. But They've had practice, over the centuries.'

'Go on,' Crow prompted when the horror that housed Wendy-Smith's mind paused. 'Why did they keep your brain alive?'

'So that They could . . . *glug* . . . milk it, drain off its knowledge bit by bit. I was known as a learned man, gentlemen. I . . . *glug-glug* . . . had knowledge of all sorts of things. Knowledge which They wanted. And my knowledge was immediately to hand. They didn't have to . . . *glug* . . . employ dreams to get what They wanted.'

112

'Knowledge?' I prompted, steadier now. 'What sort of knowledge? What did they want to know?'

'. . . *Glug* . . . locations. The locations of mines – especially inoperative mines – like those at Harden and Greetham. Drilling operations, like the Yorkshire Moors Project and the North-Sea search for gas and oil. Details of city and town populations . . . *glug* . . . of scientific progress in atomics, and – '

'Atomics?' Crow again cut in. 'Why atomics? And another thing – Harden has only become inoperative *since* your . . . transition. And in your day there was no North-Sea search in progress; nor was there a Yorkshire Moors Project. You're lying!'

'No, no . . . *glug* . . . I mention these things because they are the modern counterparts of details They wanted at that time. I have only learned of these later developments through Their minds. They are in constant contact. Even now . . .'

'And atomics?' Crow repeated, apparently satisfied for the moment with the initial answer.

'I can't answer that. I only . . . *glug* . . . know *what* They are interested in, not *why*. Over the years They have drained it all from my mind. All I know, everything. Now I have nothing . . . *glug* . . . that They are interested in . . . *glug* . . . and this is the end. I thank God!' The horror in the chair paused. Its swaying and nodding became wilder in the flickering light.

'Now I must be . . . going.'

'Going? But *where*?' I babbled. 'Back to – Them?'

'No . . . *glug, glug, glug* . . . not back to Them. That is all . . . *glug* . . . over. I feel it. And They are angry. I have said too much. A few minutes more and I'll be . . . *glug* . . . free!' The pitiful horror climbed slowly to its feet, sloping somehow to one side, stumbling and barely managing to keep its balance.

Titus Crow, too, started to his feet. 'Wait, you can help us! You must know what they fear. We need to know. We need weapons against them!'

'*Glug, glug, glug* – no time – They have released Their control over this . . . *glug* . . . body! The protoplasm is . . . *glug, glug, ggglug* . . . falling apart! I'm sorry, Crow . . . *gluggg, aghhh* . . . I'm sorry.'

Now the thing was collapsing in upon itself and waves of monstrous, venomous fetor were issuing from it. It was swaying from side to side and stumbling to and fro, visibly spreading at its base and thinning at its top, melting like an icicle beneath the blast of a blowtorch.

'Atomics, yes! *Glugggg, urghhh, achhh-achhh!* You may be . . . *gluggg* . . . right! Ludwig Prinn, on . . . *gluggg-ughhh* . . . on Azathoth!'

The stench was now intolerable. Fumes of black vapour were actually *pouring* from the staggering, melting figure by the open door. I followed Crow's lead, hastily cramming a handkerchief to my nose and mouth. The horror's last words – a gurgled shriek – before it collapsed in upon itself and sloped across the planking of the floor, were these:

'Yes, Crow . . . *glarghhh, arghhh, urghhh* . . . look to Prinn's *De Vermis Mysteriis*!'

In a matter of seconds then, there was merely a spreading stain on the floor – but, God help me, within the pattern of that stain was a hideously suggestive lump!

A human brain in an alien, protoplasmic body!

I was paralysed, I don't mind admitting it, but Crow had leaped into action. Already the paraffin-lamp was back to full power, filling the cabin with light, and suddenly my friend's commands were echoing in my ears:

'Out, de Marigny. Out on to the gangplank. The stench is positively poisonous!' He half pushed me, half dragged me out through the door and into the clean night air. I sat down on the gangplank and was sick, horribly sick, into the obscenely chuckling river.

Crow, though, however affected he was or had been by the occurrences of the last half hour, had quickly regained control of himself. I heard the latticed cabin windows being thrown open, heard Crow's strangled coughing as he moved about in the noisome interior, heard his footsteps and laboured breathing as he came out on deck and crossed to the other side to fling something – something which splashed loudly – into the flowing river.

Too, as my sickness abated, I heard him drawing water and the sounds of his swilling down the cabin floor. I thanked my lucky stars I had not, as had once been my intention, had the cabin carpeted! A fresh breeze had sprung up to assist greatly in removing from the *Seafree* the poisonous taint of our visitor, and by the time I was able to get back on my feet it was plain that the houseboat would soon be back to normal.

It was then, just before midnight, as Crow came back on deck in his shirt sleeves, that a taxi pulled up on the river path level with the gangplank. Crow and I watched as the passenger alighted with a large briefcase and as, in the glow from the rear lights, a suitcase was taken from the boot. Plainly I heard the newcomer's voice as he paid his fare:

'I thank you very much. They're in, I see, so there'll be no need to wait.'

There was the merest trace of cultured, North American accent to that dignified voice, and I saw the puzzled look on Crow's face deepen as the second visitor of that fateful night made his way carefully to the foot of the gangplank. The taxi pulled away into the night.

'Hello, there,' the newcomer called as he stepped up the sloping walkway towards us. 'Mr Titus Crow, I believe – and Mr Henri-Laurent de Marigny?'

As he came into the light I saw an elderly gentleman whose grey hair went well with his intelligent, broad-browed head and wide, searching eyes. His clothes, I saw, were cut in the most conservative American style.

'You have us at a disadvantage, sir,' said Crow, carefully holding out his hand in greeting.

'Ah, of course.' The stranger smiled. 'Please forgive me. We've never met, you and I, but we've found a number of occasions in the past on which to correspond!'

For a moment my friend's frown deepened even further, but then the light of recognition suddenly lit in his eyes and he gasped as he gripped the other's hand more firmly. 'Then you'll be – '

'Peaslee,' the newcomer said. 'Wingate Peaslee of Miskatonic, and I'm delighted to make your acquaintance.'

8

Peaslee of Miskatonic

(From de Marigny's Notebooks)

Never before in my life had I experienced a night of such revelation.

Peaslee had flown in from America as soon as he got Crow's first letter, setting out from the university in Arkham even before the arrival of the eggs, which would now be put to certain as yet unspecified *uses* in America. Upon his arrival in London, he had tried to get in touch with Crow by telephone, eventually contacting the Reverend Harry Townley. But even then he had had to present himself at the reverend's residence, with such credentials as he had with him, before he could learn of Crow's whereabouts. Our ecclesiastical doctor friend was not one to neglect a trust!

'Solid as a rock,' Crow said when he heard this. 'Good old Harry!'

Once the reverend had cleared Peaslee, then he had told the professor of my own involvement in Crow's 'mysterious' activities. Though one of his prime objectives in journeying to England was to see Crow, he was not displeased at my presence or at my participation in my friend's adventures. He had heard much of my father – the Great New Orleans mystic, Etienne-Laurent de Marigny – and assumed correctly from the beginning that much of the paternal personality, particularly the love of obscure and macabre mysteries, had rubbed off on me.

He had come, he told us, among other things to welcome us into the membership of an organization, or rather, a 'Foundation', the Wilmarth Foundation. The direction of this unofficial institute was under Peaslee's own control – his and that of an administrative board formed by certain of Miskatonic's older, more experienced professors – and the Foundation's formation proper had been initiated after the untimely death of the sage for whom it was named. Its prime aim was to carry out the work that old Wilmarth, before his death, had stated he wished to commence.

Peaslee recognized immediately and was amazed at Crow's erudition regarding the Cthulhu Cycle of myth (mine to a lesser degree); and, once Titus had mentioned them in conversation, pressed him for details of his prophetic dreams. It appeared he knew of other men with Crow's strange brand of 'vision'; a somnambulant psyche, as it were! But the professor's own revelations were by far the night's most astounding, and his fascinating conversation was to carry us well into the early hours of the next day.

Before he would even begin to explain in detail, however, his unforeseeable arrival at the houseboat, seeing our obvious state of distress, he demanded to know all that had passed since the Harden eggs came into Crow's hands. In the earlier occurrences of the night in particular, Peaslee was interested – not in any morbid sense or out of grotesque curiosity, but because this was a facet of the Cthonians of which he knew nothing: their ability to preserve the identity of their victim by prisoning the brain in living tissues of their own construction. He carefully made notes as we told him of our awful, pitiful visitor, and only when he knew the most minute of the horrific details was he satisfied.

Then, and with considerable attention to detail – if occasionally prodded by our eager questions – he told us of the Wilmarth Foundation; of its inception at the deathbed of his one-time companion in dark and legendary arcana; of its resultant recruitment of scores of dedicated men – the 'horror-hunters' as foreseen by Sir Amery Wendy-Smith – and of their now almost worldwide organization aimed at the ultimate destruction of all the extant Cthulhu Cycle deities.

But before I go into Peaslee's fantastic disclosures too deeply, I feel I should make plain the truly astonishing sensations of *relief* enjoyed both by Titus Crow and myself from the moment the professor set foot aboard *Seafree*. If I had thought before that Crow had 'freed' me with his chantings and splashings on that morning when the Cthonians had held me in their mental grasp – well, what was I to make of this new and fuller feeling of mental and physical freeness? The harsh lines on the face of Titus Crow lifted in less than half an hour, his unaccustomed nervousness gave way to an almost euphoric gayness quite out of character even in his lightest moments; and as for myself – why, I had not known such sheer joie de vivre for years, for longer than I could remember, and this despite my surroundings and the horror they had known only a few short hours earlier. Without Peaslee's explanation for this mental uplifting – which did not come, except as a hint, until later – it was far from obvious whence these sensations sprang. He did eventually clear up the matter for us (after my friend and I had remarked once or twice upon this remarkable and sudden exhilaration) with an explanation both enlightening and gratifying. At last, it seemed, Crow and I were to have the penultimate protection against the Cthonians, and against their mind- and dream-sendings. For although we had not known it, even with Crow's expert use of the Vach-Viraj Incantation and the Tikkoun Elixir, the Cthonian mastery of dreams and subconscious mind and mental telepathy had still held over us at least the echoes of their evil influence. Only the Elder Gods themselves had ultimate power – and, even if it were known how, what man would dare conjure *them*? Would they even permit such a conjuring? Everyone, Peaslee had it, was subject to the influence of the forces of evil to one degree or another, but there was a solution to such moods and states of psychic depression. We were, as I have said, later to learn what that solution was.

The professor's reason for coming to England, as he had already half stated, was not wholly to invite Titus Crow into the company of the Wilmarth Foundation; but on receipt of Crow's letter he had realized at once that its author desperately needed his help – his *immediate* help, if it was not to be Wendy-Smith and Wilmarth all over again!

He explained how Professor Albert N. Wilmarth, long interested in and an authority on Fortian and macabre occurrences, especially those connected with the Cthulhu Cycle of myth, had died quietly following a long illness many years ago. At the height of this illness Wendy-Smith was sending Wilmarth imploring telegrams – telegrams which, because of his comatose condition at the time, the ailing professor was never able to answer! On his partial recovery and not long before his relapse, slow decline, and eventual death, he had blamed his English colleague's monstrous demise on himself. Then, while he was able, Wilmarth had gathered to him all references available in literature to the subterranean beings of the Cthulhu Cycle. Upon receipt of a copy of the Wendy-Smith manuscript (before its first publication in alleged 'fiction' form), he had taken it upon himself to form the nucleus of that Foundation which now secretly spanned the greater part of the Earth. Shortly thereafter he died.

Peaslee told us of the Foundation's early years, of the scepticism with which Wilmarth's posthumous report was at first met, of the subsequent explorations, scientific experiments, and researching which had gone to prove the elder 'eccentric's' theories, and of the gradual buildup of a dedicated army. Now there were almost five hundred of them – men in every walk of life, who, having chanced upon manifestations of subterranean horror or other signs of alien presences, were members of the Wilmarth Foundation – a body sworn to protect its individual members, to secretly seek out and destroy all the elder evils of Avernus, to remove for ever from the Earth the ancient taint of Cthulhu, Yog-Sothoth, Shudde-M'ell, Nyogtha, Yibb-Tstll, and all the others of the deities, their minions, and spawn.

The great occult books had early been researched, studied endlessly by sincere and single-minded men until each clue, every pointer, all references and allusions were known to the horror-hunters by heart – and then the hunt had begun in earnest.

But before all this had got under way those Demogorgons of the mythology, the Cthonians, had spread into many areas (although Africa was still their true stronghold), until the spawn of Shudde-M'ell was seeded far and wide, throughout all Asia, Europe, Russia, even China and Tibet. Finally, as lately as 1964, and against all the efforts of the Wilmarth Foundation, the Americas themselves had been invaded. Not that this invasion constituted the first dealings of these beings of elder myth and their minions with the Americas. On the contrary; the United States particularly – and especially the New England seaboard – had known diverse forms of the horrors many times, and Their presence in the domed hills and wooded valleys of that area was immemorially recorded and predated the very Indians and their forebears. This was the first time, however, that Shudde-M'ell's kind had gained a foothold upon (or rather, *within*) the North American landmass!

Crow had found this invasion just a fraction too hard to understand, until Peaslee reminded him of the Cthonian ability to get into the minds of men. There were, beyond a doubt, people temporarily and even permanently in the employ of the burrowers beneath – usually men of weak character or low breeding and mental characteristics – and such persons had transported eggs to the United States for the further propagation of the horrors! These mental slaves of the Cthonians had, on a number of occasions, attempted to infiltrate the Foundation – had even tried to get inside Miskatonic University itself. But again the as yet unspecified 'protections' of Foundation members had been sufficient to ward off such deluded men. After all, their minds were in effect the minds of the Cthonians, and therefore that same power which worked against all Cthulhu Cycle deities worked against them!

The main trouble in dealing with Shudde-M'ell's sort (Peaslee was quite matter-of-fact in his treatment of the theme) was that any method used against them could more often than not only be used once. Their telepathic contact with one another – and, indeed, with others of the mythology – was of course instantaneous. This meant that should a means be employed to destroy one nest of the creatures, then it was more than likely that the other nests knew of it immediately and would avoid any such similar treatment. Thanks to Miskatonic's technical theorists, researchers, and experimentalists, however, an as yet untried plan had been formulated to destroy certain of the earth-dwelling types of the CCD (Peaslee's abbreviation for Cthulhu Cycle deities) without alerting other of the horrors. This plan was now scheduled for use both in England as well as America. Preparations had already been made for the initial American experiment, which would now have to be delayed until arrangements could be made for a simultaneous attack upon the Cthonian nests of Britain. Crow and I, as members of the Wilmarth Foundation, would see the results of this project.

While the professor was sketching in the details of these facts for us, I could see Crow growing more restless and eager to speak by the second. Sure enough, as soon as Peaslee paused for a breath, he put in: 'Then there *are* known ways of killing these things?'

'Certainly, my friends' – the professor looked at us both – 'and if your minds hadn't been so fogged over these last few weeks I'm sure you would have discovered some of them for yourselves. Most of the earth-dwelling types – such as Shudde-M'ell and his lot – can be done away with simply by the use of water. They corrode, rot, and evaporate in water. Their internal organs break down and their pressure-mechanisms cease to function. Their makeup is more alien than you can possibly imagine. A sustained jet of water, or immersion for any appreciable length of time, is quite fatal; and there's damn little left to look at afterwards! It's strange, I know, that Shudde-M'ell's ultimate striving is towards freeing Great Cthulhu – which the Foundation, in Wendy-Smith's footsteps, believes – for Cthulhu would appear essentially to be the greatest of the *water*-elementals. The fact of the matter is, though, that R'lyeh once stood on dry land, possibly has on a number of occasions, and that the ocean now forms the very walls of Cthulhu's prison. It is the water, thank God, that keeps down his monstrous dream-sendings to a bearable level. Even so, you'd be surprised how many inmates of the world's lunatic asylums owe their confinement to the mad call of Cthulhu. Of course, dreaming as he is in Deep R'lyeh – wherever that hellish submarine city of distant aeons hides – he is served in his slumbers by Dragons and the Deep Ones; but these in the main are creatures more truly of the great waters. Water is their element.'

'Cthulhu in fact lives, then?' Crow asked.

'Most assuredly. There are some occultists who believe him to be dead, I am told, but – '

'"That is not dead which can eternal lie . . ."' Crow finished for him, quoting the first line of Alhazred's much discussed couplet.

'Exactly,' Peaslee agreed.

'I know a different version of it,' I said.

'Oh?' The professor cocked his head at me.

'"That which is alive hath known death, and that which is dead yet can never die, for in the Circle of the Spirit life is naught and death is naught. Yea, all things live for ever, though at times they sleep and are forgotten."'

Crow raised his eyebrows in question, but before he could speak I said: 'From the ninth chapter of H. Rider Haggard's *She*, from the lips of a hideous phoenix in a dream.'

'Ah, but you'll find many allusions and parallels in fiction, Henri,' Peaslee told me. 'Particularly in that type of fiction so marvellously typified in Haggard. I suppose you could say that Ayesha was a fire-elemental.'

'Talking of elementals' – Crow entered the conversation – 'you say that many of the earth-types rot in water. Now, you say it as if you'd actually seen such a . . . a *dissolution* – but how can you be so sure?'

'Dissolution, you say. Hmmm,' Peaslee mused. 'No, more an incredibly rapid *catabolism*, I would say. And yes, I have seen such a thing. Three years ago we hatched an egg at Miskatonic.'

'What?' Crow cried. 'Wasn't that a very dangerous thing to do?'

'Not at all,' Peaslee answered, unflustered. 'And it was quite necessary. We had to study the things, Crow – as much as Earthly knowledge would allow. We still are studying them. It's all very well to theorize and conjecture, but practice is the only way. So we hatched an egg.

We've done it often since then, I assure you! But this first one: we had it in a large boxlike room, a pentagonal room with an imprisoning device set in the centre of each of the five walls. Oh, the thing was well and truly prisoned, both physically and mentally; it could neither move from its room nor communicate with others of its kind! We fed it mainly on soil and basaltic gravel. Oh, yes, we tried it on the flesh of dead animals, too, which produced a hideous blood-lust in it – and so it was obviously safer to feed the thing on minerals. At only six months old the creature was as fat as two men around and nine feet long; like a great grey ugly squid. It wasn't full-grown by any means, but nevertheless we were satisfied that it was at least big enough to accommodate our experiments. We had a good idea that water might do the trick. Even old Wendy-Smith' – he paused momentarily to peer with horror-shrouded eyes, nonetheless wonderingly, even calculatingly, at the now faint stains on the floorboards – 'knew that much, and so we left the water-test until the last. Acids didn't seem to worry it in the slightest, or any but the most extreme degrees of heat – and we used a laser! Nor, as we'd expected, did pressure, shock, or blast affect it; even powerful explosives set off *in contact* with the thing didn't bother it unnecessarily, other than forcing it to fill in the gaps blown in its protoplasm! Water, though, did the trick beautifully. But before that there was one other thing we tried, and it worked so well that we had to stop the treatment or simply kill the thing out of hand.'

'Oh?' Crow questioned. 'Might I hazard a guess before you tell us?'

'Certainly.'

'Radiation,' my friend said with certainty. 'The thing did not like radiation!'

Peaslee seemed surprised. 'Quite correct. But how did you know?'

'There are two clues,' Crow answered. 'One, the eggs of these creatures are shielded against radiation; and two, there was that which Sir Amery – or rather his brain in that monstrous body – told us before he . . . *it* . . . died.'

'Eh?' I cast my mind swiftly back.

'Yes,' said Crow. 'He said that we might "try Ludwig Prinn on Azathoth." And of course Azathoth is the "Nuclear Chaos" of the Cthulhu Cycle.'

'Good,' said Peaslee, obviously appreciative of my friend's grasp of the matter, 'and do you know the passage in *De Vermis Mysteriis* to which Wendy-Smith referred?'

'No, but I'm aware that there's a so-called "invocation" in the book for raising Azathoth temporarily.'

'There is indeed' – Peaslee nodded his head grimly – 'one which bears out your theory – and that of the Wilmarth Foundation, incidentally – that the "magic" of the Elder Gods was in fact super-science. It is a spell involving the use of an unspecified metal, one which, to use Prinn's own words, "may be found only by the most powerful use of extreme and dangerous thaumaturgies." He even gave the required amount of this metal, but in cryptic terms. We sorted out his symbols, though, using the university computer, and discovered his principal measurements. The rest was easy. Prinn had in fact specified a critical mass of highly fissionable material!'

'An atomic explosion!' Crow gasped.

'Of course,' Peaslee agreed.

'But there are many such "invocations" in the great Black Books – the *Necronomicon* and others of its kind,' Crow protested.

'Yes, and some of them are vocal neutralizers of the mind-prisons of the Elder Gods. In most cases, thank God, their pronunciation is a veritable impossibility. Yes, we can count ourselves as damned lucky that the ancients, particularly Alhazred, didn't have a system of getting the pronunciation of many of these things down on paper – or papyrus, or stone, or whatever. Also, it's fortunate that man's vocal cords are not naturally given to the use of such alien syllables!'

'But wait,' Crow cried in apparent exasperation. 'Here we have decided that Azathoth is nothing more than a nuclear explosion, a destructive device *against* the CCD. But surely he was the original *leader* of the Great Old Ones, including Cthulhu, in their rebellion against the Elder Gods? I don't follow.'

'Don't take the old writings too much at their face value, Titus,' the professor told him. 'For instance: think of Azathoth as he/it is described – "an amorphous blight of nethermost confusion which blasphemes and bubbles at the centre of all infinity"; that is, central in time and space. Now, given that time and space support each other's existence, they therefore commenced initially simultaneously; and because Azathoth is coexistent with all time and conterminous in all space *he was there at the beginning!* This is in effect how he became the first rebel – he altered the perfect negative-structure of a timeless spacelessness into the chaotic continuum which we have today. Consider his nature, Titus: a "nuclear chaos". Why, he was – he *is* – nothing less than the Big Bang itself, and to hell with your Steady-State theorists!'

'The Big Bang,' Crow repeated, patently in awe of the vision Peaslee had conjured.

'Of course.' The professor nodded. 'Azathoth, who "created this Earth", and who, it is foretold in books predating mere man, "shall destroy it when the seals are broken." Oh, yes, Titus – and this isn't the only mythos that has us going in flames next time!' He paused to let this last sink in, then continued:

'But if you insist on looking at the Cthulhu Cycle literally, without admitting this sort of cryptic reference,

127

then consider this: following the failure of their rebellion, the Great Old Ones were served punishments. Azathoth was blinded and bereft of mind and will. Now, a madman is unpredictable, Titus. He rarely recognizes either friend or foe. And a *blind* madman has even less recognition. How unpredictable, then, a blind, mad chaos of nuclear reactions?'

While Peaslee had been talking, it had grown plain to me that something else was bothering Crow. He let the professor finish, then said:

'But listen here, Wingate. I accept all you say, *gladly*; I thank our lucky stars that you're here to help us out of a hole – but surely all we've done up to now is alert the CCD of your presence! All this talking, particularly what's been said about water and atomics as weapons – surely we've been giving the whole show away?'

'Not at all.' The erudite Peaslee smiled. 'True, in the beginning, when the Foundation first got started, we did give lots of information away in this manner – '

'What manner?' I cut in, having been lost by the conversation. 'Do you mean that the Cthonians can listen in on our discussions?'

'Of course, Henri,' Crow answered. 'I thought that was understood. They're good at "receiving" as well as "sending", you know!'

'Then why didn't they know where we were without first having to find you in that dream last night? Why didn't they pick your plans to come down here to Henley right out of your mind?'

Crow sighed patiently and said: 'Don't forget that we have had the use of certain protections, Henri – the Tikkoun Elixir, the Vach-Viraj Incantation. Nevertheless,' he continued, frowning, 'that's just exactly what I was getting at!'

He turned to Peaslee. 'Well, how about it, Wingate?

Here in the houseboat, while admittedly I've been using the Vach-Viraj Incantation pretty regularly, well, we've lately run out of the Tikkoun Elixir. So what's to have stopped the Cthonians from listening in on us?'

'These devices you mention are poor protections, my friend,' the professor answered. 'Perhaps they helped a little, but obviously the burrowers were still getting through to you – both of you – at least partially. It's my guess that they've known where you were all along. They are *not* getting through now, however, as witness your alert minds and, despite lack of sleep, your newfound feelings of psychic and physical freedom. Now listen:

'As I was saying, when first the Foundation got under way, we did give away lots of information in this manner, and with the passage of time the would-be hunters almost became the hunted!

'In 1958 no fewer than seven recruits of the Wilmarth Foundation met untimely, unnatural deaths, and the remaining members immediately sought protection. Of course, it had long been known that the star-stones of ancient Mnar formed the perfect barrier – certainly against their minions, to a lesser degree against the CCD themselves – but these stones were so few and far between, and usually only accidentally acquired. A definite source and supply became imperative.

'In '59 Miskatonic's kilns actually commenced manufacturing the stones – or rather, soapstone-porcelain duplicates – a process perfected by our young Professor Sandys, and by 1960 all members of the Foundation were equipped with them. The very first man-made stones were useless, by the way, but it was soon discovered that by incorporating fragments of a few damaged original stars in the composition of the manufactured ones, as many as a hundred new star-stones – each as effective as the originals – could be made from one of the old!'

Peaslee paused here to dig into his great briefcase. 'Here, by the way, are the reasons you no longer have anything to fear from the Cthonians, neither physically nor mentally . . . so long as you're careful, that is! Always remember – they *never* stop trying! You must carry these things wherever you go from now on, but even so you must try not to venture anywhere below the surrounding ground-level. I mean that you're to keep out of valleys, gulleys, quarries, mines, subways, and so on. As I've said, you needn't fear a direct attack, but they can still get at you indirectly. A sudden earthquake, a fall of rock – I'm sure you follow my meaning.'

He produced two small packages which he carefully unwrapped, passing the contents of one to Crow and the other to me. 'I have many more of them. These two, however, are yours personally from now on. They should keep you out of trouble.'

I examined the thing in my hand. It was of course a star-stone, featureless, grey-green; the thing might easily have been a small, fossil starfish. Crow, too, gave his stone a thoughtful examination, then said: 'So these are the star-stones of ancient Mnar.'

'Yes,' Peaslee agreed. 'Except you couldn't call *these* stones exactly ancient. They are samples from Miskatonic's kilns – but for all that, they're just as powerful as the real things.'

Crow carefully placed his stone in the inside pocket of his jacket, hanging by his bunk, then turned to thank Peaslee for what could only be called a priceless gift. He followed this up with: 'You were talking about the Wilmarth Foundation and its work. I was very interested.'

'Of course,' the professor agreed. 'Yes, we'd better get through as much as we can of basic explanations and details for tonight' – he glanced at his watch – 'or rather, this morning! We'll have to be on our way later today. Now where was I? Ah, yes!

'Well, 1959 was a momentous year for the Foundation, for as well as our discovery of a means of manufacturing these protective devices, we also sent out our first real expeditions since the 30s. The new expeditions were, though, less well advertised – almost secretive, in fact, and necessarily so – and fronted with fictitious objectives. We were particularly interested in Africa, where it was known that at least one Cthonian species – namely the kith and kin of Shudde-M'ell – were free and roaming loose. There, on the borders of that region explored by the ill-fated Wendy-Smith Expedition, our horror-hunters discovered two tribes whose members wore about their necks exhumed star-stones, protections against "evil spirits". Their witch doctors, the only members of the tribes allowed into the taboo territories, had been digging up the stones immemorially, and the *Mganga* with the greatest number of stars to his credit was reckoned a very powerful witch doctor indeed. Witch doctors, it may be added, did not have a great life expectancy in that area. Inevitably they would dig where they ought not!

'Incidentally, this ritual collecting of the star-stones explains Shudde-M'ell's original escape from those prisoning environs, and how his brethren were liberated to pursue their aeon-old policy of regeneration, infiltration, and their efforts to free even worse horrors throughout the world. The throne-nest had remained in G'harne for some time after the general exodus, it seemed, but it was members of the nest that followed Wendy-Smith back to England. Now, of course, as you are only too well aware, England has its own loathsome complement of the Cthonians.

'Wendy-Smith was a bit confused as to their propagative rate, though. He speaks of "hordes", then of "extremely slow procreative processes". In fact, the creatures *are* slow in producing – but not all that slow! We can reckon on a cycle of thirty years, with a female laying two to four eggs at a time. The trouble is that once they've reached this thirty-year stage of maturity they can lay every ten years. By the time a female has reached her century she may very well have littered thirty-two pups! Fortunately, so far as we've been able to ascertain, only one in every eight of these monstrous "children" is female. I rather fancy that one of the G'harne eggs which Wendy-Smith unknowingly took was just such a female!' The professor let this ominous thought sink in, then added: 'Overall, I should think we can take it that some hundreds of the beings are now alive and spreading.'

'This is fascinating,' Crow murmured. 'How do you track them down, Peaslee – what system do you employ to detect the beasts?'

'Initially, as your English professor suggested, we tried specialized seismological equipment, but the system wasn't accurate enough. For example: how might one tell a "natural" from an "unnatural" tremor? Of course, we also have a worldwide news service, and our headquarters at Miskatonic is ever on the lookout for inexplicable disappearances or anything else suggesting the involvement of the CCD. For the last few years, though, we've been using people gifted as you yourself, Crow, are gifted.'

'Eh?' My friend was taken aback. 'Gifted like me? I fail to see what you're getting at, Peaslee.'

'Why, your *dreams*, my friend! Even though you were not then "on the books", as it were, of the CCD, still you picked up impressions from their monstrous minds. To a degree – certainly on the Cthonian thought-levels – you're telepathic, Crow! And, as I've said, you're not alone in your ability.'

132

'Of course,' I cried, snapping my fingers. 'But that explains why I came back from France, Titus! I could sense that something was wrong; I knew that somehow I was being *called* back to England. Furthermore, it explains my moods of depression in the weeks prior to your inviting me in on this thing – I was picking up the echoes of your own gloom!'

Peaslee was immediately interested, and made me relate to him all of my doom-fraught sensations throughout the period leading up to my return from Paris, 'as though drawn back', to London.

When I was done, he said, 'Then it seems we must acknowledge you, too, de Marigny, as being something of a telepath. You may not be able to project your thoughts and emotions, as Crow here obviously can, but you can certainly *receive* such sendings! Good – it seems that the Foundation has recruited two more extremely valuable members.'

'Do you mean to say,' Crow pressed, 'that you're using telepaths to track these creatures down?'

'Yes, we are. It is easily the most successful phase of all our operations,' the professor answered.

'And yet' – Crow seemed puzzled – 'you haven't discovered the whereabouts of R'lyeh, Cthulhu's seat at the bottom of the sea?'

'What? You surprise me!' Peaslee seemed shocked. 'Do you really think we'd risk men by asking them to contact Cthulhu?' He frowned. 'And yet, in fact . . . there was one of our telepaths who took it upon himself to do just that. He was a "dreamer", just like you, and he was on a nonaddictive drug we've developed to induce deep sleep. But on one occasion, well, he didn't follow orders. Left a note explaining what he was trying to do. All very laudable – and very stupid! He's in a Boston asylum now; hopeless case.'

'Good God . . . of course!' Crow gasped as the implications hit him. 'He *would* be!'

'Yes,' Peaslee grimly agreed. 'Anyhow, this method of ours of using telepaths didn't evolve properly until two years ago, but now we've developed it fully. I flew over here yesterday in the company of one of our telepaths, and later today he'll be off to look up a British colleague – a pilot, ostensibly in "Ordnance Survey". They'll hire a small aeroplane, and tomorrow or the day after they'll start quartering England, Scotland, and Wales.'

'Quartering?' I asked.

'It's our term for dividing into a series of squares an area to be "prospected",' Peaslee explained. 'David Winters – that's the telepath's name – can detect a CCD up to a distance of twenty-five miles; he can *pinpoint* them from five miles away! In a matter of a week or two we'll know the location of every nest and each individual horror in all three countries – if all goes according to plan.'

'And Ireland?' I asked.

'We have no reason to believe that the Emerald Isle has yet been invaded,' the professor answered. 'Ireland will, though, be checked over at a later date.'

'But they can *move*!' Crow protested. 'By the time your telepath has done with his job, his early, er – sightings? – could be a hundred miles away from where he first plotted them!'

'That's true,' Peaslee agreed, unperturbed, 'but we're after *numbers*, mainly, and large concentrations. We have to know the best spots to start drilling, you see?'

Crow and I, both equally baffled by this new phase of the professor's revelations, looked at one another in consternation. 'No,' I eventually answered. 'I don't think we do see.'

'Let me explain,' Peaslee offered. 'We have men with the big companies; with Seagasso, Lescoil, the NCB, ICI,

Norgas, even in govermental circles. Now a few of these men are Americans, trained at Miskatonic and slotted in over here when opportunities presented themselves, but most are of course natives of Great Britain contacted and recruited over the years through the machinery of the Wilmarth Foundation. We have, too, interested parties in certain ministries: such as the Ministry of Land and Development, Agriculture and Fisheries, National Resources, etc.

'The "Great Britain Operation", as we call it, has been planned for some years now, but when this opportunity came along – that is, the opportunity to do a bit of incidental, valuable recruiting, as well as to intervene in what might well have turned out to be a very nasty affair – well, it seemed to me that this was the perfect time to put the plan into operation.

'I will in fact supervise and coordinate the project in its entirety. You two gentlemen will no doubt be able to help me tremendously in this, and learn a lot about the Foundation's workings at the same time. For instance, though these may seem relatively minor points to you, I don't like the idea of driving on the left, I'm not at all sure of your British road signs, and I'm damned if I'll be driven around for the next few months in a cab! The latter's out of the question, anyway, for we'll be seeing some pretty strange things before we're through, and the presence of a cabdriver is just not acceptable. Obviously, the public must be kept in the dark about all this. We'll need a large automobile – '

'I have a Mercedes garaged at Henley,' Crow hastily put in.

'And of course I'll need someone with a good knowledge of British geography, topography, and so on. All of which is where you gentlemen should come in very nicely,' Peaslee finished.

'But wait,' I dazedly protested, one part of my mind following the conversation, another groping at what had gone before. 'You were talking about *drilling*!'

'Ah, yes! So I was. I'm often guilty of a little mental wandering when I'm a bit weary. You'll excuse me, de Marigny, but I've a lot on my mind and these details are just routine to me. Drilling, yes – well, the plan is this: once we've ascertained where the nests are, we'll choose two or three centrally situated drilling sites as far out of the way of the general public as we can manage, and then we'll commence the drilling of our star-wells – '

'Star-wells?' this, again, was from me.

'Yes, that's what we call them. Deep shafts to accommodate star-stones. We drill five equally spaced star-wells in a great circle some hundreds of yards across, and one central hole to take the eggs. The idea is that once we let the eggs down the central shaft – until which time, incidentally, they'll be kept "prisoned" by the proximity of star-stones so that local adults will not know of their whereabouts – we can expect the adults to come burrowing to the rescue. Of course, their rescue attempt will fail! As soon as our telepaths and instruments tell us of the arrival of a sufficiently large number of the adult creatures . . . then we'll let down the star-stones into the perimeter wells. All the Cthonians within the circle will be trapped.'

'But these creatures can move in three dimensions, you know, Wingate,' Crow pointed out. 'Surely your star-stones will be lying on a strictly two-dimensional plane? What's to stop the adult Cthonians from simply burrowing straight down – or worse still . . . *up*?'

'No, the circle ought to be sufficient, Titus. We've experimented, as I've said – you remember what I told you of the eggs we hatched? – and we're pretty sure that our plan is sound. What we might do, if we're lucky enough to be able to get our hands on them at the right time, is this: instead of using eggs we'll use young female creatures! They'll provide a sure draw. And then, well, even if the adults do try to make an escape after we lower the star-stones, it will be far too late!'

Crow held up his hands and shook his head. 'Hold on a minute, Peaslee! First off, where will you get your young females; and secondly, why will any attracted adults be "too late" to get away?' Doubt was showing on my friend's face again.

'As to your first question,' the professor answered, 'we have a regular hatchery at Miskatonic. We took two dozen eggs from G'harne, and we've collected others since then. That's where your four eggs are destined for, by the way. Your second question? Well, as soon as the adults appear on the scene and after we've set the star-stones in place – then we flood the whole underground area by pumping water down the shafts under high pressure!'

For a moment there was silence, then Crow said: 'And you say there'll be a number of these sites?'

'Yes, and the timings for the operations will of course be perfectly synchronized – simply to ensure that if the Cthonians do manage to get "distress signals" out past the star-stones, well, at least we'll have cleaned out a large number of them at one swipe. In that event, it would mean searching for a new plan of attack for later projects, but . . .' Peaslee frowned thoughtfully for a moment, then added: 'But anyway, after we've had this initial bash at the burrowers – then we'll be able to turn our attentions to the other British CCD.'

'*Others?*' I exploded. 'What others?' I noticed that Crow seemed less surprised.

'Well, we know that there are a number of different types of these beings, Henri, these dwellers in the deep earth,' the professor patiently explained. 'And therefore it's a fair bet that Great Britain has her share. Some, though, are apparently far more vulnerable to orthodox weapons. One of our men – an Englishman, by the way – has had a certain amount of personal experience with just such a being. This same chap is a drilling expert; a fellow known as "Pongo" Jordan, who used to be with Seagasso's oceangoing rigs. Now he's a member of the Foundation – but it took a lot of persuasion. Ostensibly, he works for Land Development. He'll be supervising the positioning of the star-wells once David Winters' report is in.'

'Jordan . . . ?' Crow mused, then looked startled. He frowned. 'Not the same Jordan who . . . And your telepath, David Winters! Well, I'll be – '

'Go on,' Peaslee said. 'Do you know Jordan and Winters?'

'I know that the Cthonians fear them desperately, as they fear you,' Crow answered. Then my friend proceeded to tell the professor of his dreams during the period when the seagoing rigs were stricken with that series of puzzling disasters, following this up with his latest nightmare wherein the Cthonians had tried to 'buy him off'.

When Crow had done, Peaslee excitedly dug into his great briefcase. 'You know, you two,' he said, 'when I first decided to fly over here, I had no idea it would be so easy to convert you to the Foundation's cause. Because of my uncertainty I gathered together certain testimonials which I hoped would help to convince you. One of these is a letter Jordan wrote to one of his superiors shortly after he lost his rig, *Sea-Maid*. Ah! Here it is. I'm sure you'll be interested to read it.'

9

The Night Sea-Maid *Went Down*

(From the Files of the Wilmarth Foundation)

Queen of the Wolds Inn
Cliffside
Bridlington, E. Yorks.
29th Nov.

J. H. Grier (Director)
Grier & Anderson
Seagasso
Sunderland, Co. Durham

Dear Johnny,

By now I suppose you'll have read my 'official' report, sent off to you from this address on the fourteenth of the month, three days after the old *Sea-Maid* went down. How I managed that report I'll never know – but anyway, I've been laid up ever since, so if you've been worried about me or wondering why I haven't let on further about my whereabouts till now, well, it hasn't really been my fault. I just haven't been up to doing much writing since the . . . disaster. Haven't been up to much of anything for that matter. God, but I hate the idea of facing a Board of Inquiry!

Anyhow, as you'll have seen from my report, I've made up my mind to quit, and I suppose it's only right I give you what I can of an explanation for my decision. After all, you've been paying me good money to manage your rigs these last four years, and no complaints there. In fact, I've no complaints period, nothing Seagasso could sort out at any rate, but I'm damned if I'll sink sea-wells again.

In fact, I'm finished with *all* prospecting! Sea, land . . . it makes no real difference now. Why, when I think of what might have happened at any time during the last four years! And now it *has* happened.

But there I go, stalling again. I'll admit right now that I've torn up three versions of this letter, pondering the results of them reaching you; but now, having thought it all out, frankly, I don't give a damn what you do with what I'm going to tell you. You can send an army of head-shrinkers after me if you like. One thing I'm sure of, though, and that's this – whatever I say won't make you suspend the North-Sea operations. 'The Country's Economy', and all that.

At least my story ought to give old Anderson a laugh; the hard, stoic, unimaginative old bastard! And no doubt about it, the story I have to tell is fantastic enough. I suppose it could be argued that I was 'in my cups' that night (and it's true enough, I'd had a few), but I can hold my drink, as you well know. Still, the facts – *as I know them* – drunk or sober, remain simply fantastic.

Now, you'll remember that right from the start there was something funny about the site off Hunterby Head. The divers had trouble; the geologists, too, with their instruments; it was the very devil of a job to float *Sea-Maid* down from Sunderland and get her anchored there; and all that was only the start of the trouble. Nevertheless, the preliminaries were all completed by early in October.

We hadn't drilled more than six hundred feet into the seabed when we brought up that first star-shaped thing. Now, Johnny, you know something? I wouldn't have given two damns for the thing, except I'd seen one before. Old Chalky Gray (who used to be with the Lescoil rig, *Ocean-Gem*, out of Liverpool) had sent me one only a few weeks before his platform and all the crew, including Chalky himself, went down twelve miles out from Withnersea. Somehow, when I saw what came up in the big core – that same star-shape – I couldn't help but think of Chalky and see some sort of nasty parallel. The one he'd sent me came up in a core too, you see? And *Ocean-Gem* wasn't the only rig lost that year in so-called 'freak storms'!

Now regarding those star-shaped stones, something more: I wasn't the only one to escape with my life the night *Sea-Maid* went down. No, that's not strictly true, I was the only one to live through *that night* – but there was a certain member of the team who saw what was coming and got out before it happened. And it was because of the star-thing that he went!

Joe Borszowski was the man – superstitious as hell, panicky, spooked at the sight of a mist on the sea – and when he saw the star-thing . . . !

It happened like this:

We'd drilled a difficult bore through some very hard stuff when, as I've said, a core-sample produced the first of those stars. Now, Chalky had reckoned the one he sent me to be a fossilized starfish of sorts, from a time when the North-Sea used to be warm; a very ancient thing. And I must admit that with its five-pointed shape, and being the size of a small starfish, I believed him to be correct. Anyway, when I showed this second star to old Borszowski he nearly went crackers! He swore we were in for trouble, demanded we all stop drilling right away and head for land, insisted that our location was 'accursed', and generally carried on like a mad thing without explaining why.

Well, I couldn't just leave it at that; if one of the lads was around the twist, you know (meaning Borszowski), he could well affect the whole operation, jeopardize the whole thing; especially if his madness took him at an important time. My immediate reaction was to want him

141

off the rig, but the radio had been giving us a bit of bother so that I couldn't call in Wes Atlee, the chopper pilot. Yes, I'd seriously thought of having the Pole lifted off by chopper. The gangs can be damned superstitious, as you well know, and I didn't want Joe infecting the other lads with his wild fancies. As it turned out, that sort of action wasn't necessary, for in no time at all old Borszowski was around apologizing for his outburst and trying to show how sorry he was about all the fuss he'd made. Something told me, though, that he'd been quite serious about his fears – whatever they were.

And so, to put the Pole's mind at rest (if I possibly could), I decided to have the rig's geologist, Carson, take the star to bits, have a closer look at it, and then let me know what the thing actually was. Of course, he'd tell me it was simply a fossilized starfish; I'd report the fact to Borszowski; things would be back to normal. So naturally, when Carson told me that it *wasn't* a fossil, that he didn't know exactly *what* it was – well, I kept that bit of information to myself and told Carson to do the same. I was sure that whatever the trouble was with Borszowski, well, it wouldn't be helped any by telling him that the star-thing was not a perfectly ordinary, completely explicable object.

The drilling brought up two or three more of the stars down to about a thousand feet, but nothing after that, so for a period I forgot all about them. As it happened, I should have listened a bit more willingly to the Pole – and I *would* have, too, if I'd followed my intuition.

You see, I've got to admit that I'd been spooky myself right from the start. The mists were too heavy, the sea too quiet . . . things were altogether too queer all the way down the line. Of course, I didn't experience any of the troubles the divers or geologists had known – I didn't join the rig until she was in position, ready to chew – but I was certainly in on it from then on. It had really started with the sea-phones, even before the advent of the stars.

Now, you know I'm not knocking your phones, Johnny; they've been a damn good thing ever since Seagasso developed them, giving readings right down to the inch, almost, so's we could tell just exactly when the drill was going through into gas or oil. And they didn't let us down this time, either . . . we simply failed to recognize or heed their warnings, that's all.

In fact, there were lots of warnings, but, as I've said, it started with the sea-phones. We'd put a phone down inside each leg of the rig, right on to the seabed where they sat 'listening' to the drill as it cut its way through the rocks, picking up the echoes as the steel worked its way down and the sounds of the cutting rebounded from the strata below. And, of course, everything they 'heard' was duplicated electronically and fed out to us through our computer. Which was why we believed initially that either the computer was on the blink or one of the phones was shaky. You see, even when we weren't drilling – when we were changing bits or lining the hole – we were still getting readings from the computer!

Oh, the trouble was there all right, whatever it was, but it was showing up so regularly that we were fooled into believing the fault to be mechanical. On the seismograph, it showed as a regular blip in an otherwise perfectly normal line; a blip that came up bang on time once every five seconds or so – *blip . . . blip . . . blip* – very odd! But, seeing that in every other respect the information coming out of the computer was spot on, no one worried overmuch about this inexplicable deviation. The blips were there right to the end, and it was only then that I found a reason for them, but in between there came other difficulties – not the least of them being the trouble with the fish.

143

Now, if that sounds a bit funny, well, it was a funny business. The lads had rigged up a small platform, slung twenty feet or so below the main platform and about the same height above the water, and in their off-duty hours when they weren't resting or knocking back a pint in the mess, you could usually see one or two of them down there fishing.

First time we found anything odd in the habits of the fish around the rig was one morning when Nick Adams hooked a beauty. All of three feet long, the fish was, wriggling and yellow in the cold November sunlight. Nick just about had the fish docked when the hook came out of its mouth so that it fell back among some support-girders down near where leg number four was being washed by a slight swell. It just lay there, flopping about a bit, in the girders. Nick scrambled down after it with a rope around his waist while his brother Dave hung on to the other end. And what do you think? When he got down to it, damned if the fish didn't go for him! It actually made to *bite* him, flopping after him on the girders, and snapping its jaws until he had to yell for Dave to haul him up.

Later he told us about it; how the damned thing hadn't even tried to get back into the sea, seeming more interested in setting its teeth in him than preserving its own life! Now, you'd expect that sort of reaction from a great eel, Johnny, wouldn't you? But hardly from a cod – not from a North-Sea cod!

From then on, Spellman, the diver, couldn't go down – not *wouldn't*, mind you, *couldn't* – the fish simply wouldn't let him. They'd chew on his suit, his air-hose . . . he got to be so frightened of them that he became quite useless to us. I can't see as I blame him, though, especially when I think of what later happened to Robertson.

But of course, before Robertson's accident, there was that further trouble with Borszowski. It was in the sixth week, when we were expecting to break through at any time, that Joe failed to come back off shore leave. Instead, he sent me a long, rambling explanatory letter; and to be truthful, when first I read it, I figured we were better off without him. The man had quite obviously been cracking up for a long time. He went on about *monsters*, sleeping in great caverns underground and especially under the sea, waiting for a chance to take over the surface world. He said that those star-shaped stones were seals to keep these monster beings ('gods', he called them) imprisoned; that the gods could control the weather to a degree; that they were capable of influencing the actions of lesser creatures – such as fish, or, occasionally, men – and that he believed one of them must be lying there, locked in the ground beneath the sea, pretty close to where we were drilling. He was frightened we were going to set it loose! The only thing that had stopped him from pressing the matter earlier was that then, as now, he'd believed we'd all think he was mad! Finally, though, he'd had to 'warn' me, knowing that if anything *did* happen, he'd never forgive himself if he hadn't at least tried.

Well, like I say, Borszowski's letter was rambling and disjointed – and yet, despite my first conclusion, the Pole had written the thing in a rather convincing manner. Hardly what you'd expect from a real madman. He quoted references from the Bible, particularly Exodus 20:4, and again and again emphasized his belief that the star-shaped things were nothing more or less than prehistoric pentacles laid down by some great race of alien sorcerers many millions of years ago. He reminded me of the heavy, unusual mists we'd had and of the queer way the cod had gone for Nick Adams. He even brought up

145

again the question of the shaky sea-phones and computer; making, in toto, an altogether disturbing assessment of *Sea-Maid*'s late history as applicable to his own odd fancies.

In fact, I became *so* disturbed by that letter that I was still thinking about it later that evening, and about the man himself, the superstitious Pole.

I did a little checking on Joe's background, discovering that he'd travelled far in his early days to become something of a scholar in obscure mythological matters. Also, it had been noticed on occasion – whenever the mists were heavier than usual, particularly since the appearance of the first star-stone – that he crossed himself with a strange sign over his breast. A number of the lads had seen him do it. They all told the same tale about that sign; that it was pointed, one point straight up, two more down and wide, two still lower but closer together. Yes, the Pole's sign was a five-pointed star! And again I read his letter.

By then we'd shut down for the day and I was out on the main platform having a quiet pipeful – I can concentrate, you know, with a bit of 'baccy. Dusk was only a few minutes away when the . . . *accident* . . . happened.

Robertson, the steel-rigger, was up aloft tightening a few loose bolts halfway up the rig. Don't ask me where the mist came from, I don't know, but suddenly it was there. It swam up from the sea, a thick grey blanket that cut visibility down to no more than a few feet. I'd just shouted up to Robertson, telling him that he'd better pack it in for the night, when I heard his yell and saw his lantern (he must have lit it as soon as the mist rolled in) come blazing down out of the greyness. The lantern disappeared through an open hatch, and a second later Robertson followed it. He went straight through the hatchway, missing the sides by inches, and then there came the splashes as first the lantern, then the man hit the sea. In two shakes of a dog's tail Robertson was splashing about down there in the mist and yelling fit to ruin his lungs, proving to me and the others who'd rushed out from the mess at my call that his fall had done him little harm. We lowered a raft immediately, getting two of the men down to the water in less than two minutes, and no one gave it a second thought that Robertson wouldn't be picked up. He was, after all, an excellent swimmer. In fact, the lads on the raft thought the whole episode was a big laugh . . . that is until Robertson started to scream!

I mean, there are screams and there are *screams*, Johnny! Robertson wasn't drowning – he wasn't making noises like a drowning man!

He wasn't picked up, either. No less quickly than it had settled, the mist lifted, so that by the time the raft touched water visibility was normal for a November evening . . . but there was no sign of the steel-rigger. There *was* something, though, something we'd all forgotten – for the whole surface of the sea was silver with fish!

Fish! Big and little, almost every indigenous species you could imagine. The way they were acting, apparently trying to throw themselves aboard the raft, I had the lads haul themselves back up to the platform as soon as it became evident that Robertson was gone for good. Johnny – I swear I'll never eat fish again.

That night I didn't sleep very well at all. Now, you know I'm not being callous. I mean, aboard an ocean-going rig after a hard day's work, no matter what has happened during the day, a man usually manages to sleep. Yet that night I just couldn't drop off. I kept going over in my mind all the . . . well, the *things* – the odd occurrences, the trouble with the instruments and the fish, Borszowski's letter again, and finally, of course, the

147

awful way we lost Robertson – until I thought my head must burst with the burden of wild notions and imaginings going round and round inside it.

Next afternoon the chopper came in again (with Wes Atlee complaining about having had to make two runs in two days) and delivered all the booze and goodies for the party the next day. As you know, we always have a blast aboard when we strike it rich – and this time the geological samples had more or less assured us of a good one. We'd been out of beer a few days by that time – poor weather had stopped Wes from bringing in anything but mail – and so I was running pretty high and dry. Now you know me, Johnny. I got in the back of the mess with all that booze and cracked a few bottles. I could see the gear turning from the window, and, over the edge of the platform, the sea all grey and eerie-looking, and somehow the idea of getting a load of booze inside me seemed a damn good one.

I'd been in there topping-up for over half an hour when Jeffries, my 2IC, got through to me on the telephone. He was in the instrument cabin and said he reckoned the drill would go through to 'muck' within a few more minutes. He sounded worried, though, sort of shaky, and when I asked him why this was, he didn't rightly seem able to answer – mumbled something about the instruments mapping those strange blips again, regular as ever but somehow stronger . . . closer.

About that time I first noticed the mist swirling up from the sea, a real pea-souper, billowing in to smother the rig and turn the men on the platform to grey ghosts. It muffled the sound of the gear, too, altering the metallic clank and rattle of pulleys and chains to distant, dull noises such as I might have expected to hear from the rig if I'd been in a suit deep down under the sea.

It was warm enough in the back room of the mess

there, yet unaccountably I found myself shivering as I looked out over the rig and listened to the ghost sounds of machinery and men.

That was when the wind came up. First the mist, then the wind – but I'd never before seen a mist that a good strong wind couldn't blow away! Oh, I've seen freak storms before, Johnny, but believe me this storm was *the* freak! With a capital 'F'.

She came up out of nowhere – not breaking the blanket of grey but driving it round and round like a great mad ghost – blasting the already choppy sea against the Old Girl's legs, flinging up spray to the platform's guard-rails, and generally creating havoc. I'd no sooner recovered from my initial amazement when the telephone rang again. I came away from the window, picked up the receiver to hear Jimmy Jeffries' somewhat distorted yell of triumph coming over the wires.

'We're *through*, Pongo!' he yelled. 'We're through and there's juice on the way up the bore right now!' Then his voice took the shakes again, going from wild excitement to terror in a second as the whole rig *wobbled* on its four great legs!

'Holy heaven – !' His voice screamed in my ear. '*What was that*, Pongo? The rig . . . wait – ' I heard the clatter as the telephone at the other end banged down, but a moment later Jimmy was back. 'It's not the rig,' he told me; 'the legs are steady as rocks – *it's the whole seabed!* Pongo, what's going on? Holy heaven – '

This time the telephone went completely dead as the rig moved again, jerking up and down three or four times in rapid succession, shaking everything loose inside the mess storeroom. I was just able to keep my feet. I still had the telephone in my hand, and just for a second or two it came back to life. Jimmy was screaming something incoherently into his end. I remember that I yelled for

149

him to get into a life jacket, that there was something awfully wrong and we were in for big trouble, but I'll never know if he heard me.

The rig rocked yet again, throwing me down on the floorboards among a debris of bottles, crates, cans, and packets; and there, skidding wildly about the tilting floor, I collided with a life jacket. God only knows what the thing was doing there in the storeroom – there were normally two or three on the platform and others were kept in the equipment shed, only taken out following storm warnings, which it goes without saying we hadn't had. But somehow I managed to struggle into it and make my way into the mess proper before the next upheaval.

By that time, over the roar of the wind and waves outside and the slap of wave-crests against the outer walls of the mess, I could hear a whipping of free-running pulleys and a high-pitched screaming of revving, uncontrolled gears – and there were *other* screams, too.

I admit that I was in a blind panic, crashing my way through the tumble of chairs and tables in the mess towards the door leading out on to the platform, when the greatest shock so far tilted the floor to what must have been thirty degrees and saved me any further effort. In that moment – as I flew against the door, bursting it open, and floundering out into the storm – I knew for sure that the old *Sea-Maid* was going down. Before, it had only been a possibility, a mad, improbable possibility; but now I knew for sure. Half stunned from my collision with the door, I was thrown roughly against the platform rails, to cling there for dear life in the howling, tearing wind and chill, rushing mist and spray.

And that was when I saw it!

I saw it . . . and in my utter disbelief I relaxed my hold on the rails and slid under them into the throat of that

150

banshee, demon storm that howled and tore at the trembling girders of the old *Sea-Maid*.

Even as I fell a colossal wave smashed into the rig, breaking two of the legs as though they were nothing stronger than matchsticks. The next instant I was in the sea, picked up, and swept away on the crest of that same wave. Even in the dizzy, sickening rush as the great wave hurled me aloft, I tried to spot *Sea-Maid* in the maelstrom of wind, mist, and ocean. It was futile and I gave it up in order to save all my effort for my own battle for survival.

I don't remember much after that – at least, not until I was picked up, and even that's not too clear. I do remember, though, while fighting the icy water, a dreadful fear of being eaten alive by fish; but so far as I know there were none about. I remember, too, being hauled aboard the lifeboat from a sea that was flat as a pancake and calm as a mill pond.

The next really lucid moment came when I woke up to find myself between clean sheets in a Bridlington hospital.

But there, I've held off from telling the important part, and for the same reason Joe Borszowski held off: I don't want to be thought a madman. Well, I'm *not* mad, Johnny, but I don't suppose for a single moment that you'll take my story seriously – nor, for that matter, will Seagasso suspend any of its North-Sea commitments – but at least I'll have had the satisfaction of knowing that I tried to warn you.

Now, remember if you will what Borszowski told me about great, alien beings lying asleep and imprisoned beneath the bed of the sea – evil 'gods' capable of controlling the weather and the actions of lesser creatures – and then explain the sight I saw before I found myself floundering in that mad ocean as the old *Sea-Maid* went down.

It was simply a gusher, Johnny, a gusher – but one such

as I'd never seen before in my whole life and hope never to see again! For instead of reaching the heavens in one solid black column, it *pulsed* upward, pumping up in short, strong jets at a rate of about one spurt in every five seconds – and it wasn't oil, Johnny! Oh, God, it wasn't oil! Booze or none, I swear I wasn't drunk; not so drunk as to make me *colour-blind*, at any rate.

For old Borszowski was right, there was one of those great god-things down there deep in the bed of the ocean, *and our drill had chopped right into it!*

Whatever it was, it had blood pretty much like ours – good and thick and red – and a great heart strong enough to pump that blood up the bore-hole right to the surface! Think of it, that monstrous giant of a thing down there in the rocks beneath the sea! How could we possibly have known? *How could we have guessed that right from the beginning our instruments had been working at maximum efficiency, that those odd, regular blips recorded on the seismograph had been nothing more than the beating of a great submarine heart?*

All of which explains, I hope, my resignation.

Bernard 'Pongo' Jordan
Bridlington, Yorks.

10

The Third Visitor

(From de Marigny's Notebooks)

The early morning was quite close, uncomfortable almost, so that by the time Titus Crow and I had finished with the astonishing Jordan document Peaslee had taken off his coat. He had adopted a very businesslike look, donning small-lensed spectacles, rolling up his shirt sleeves and busying himself with a number of files, notebooks, and various other papers from his briefcase. He was past his tired peak, he told us, and having slept on the plane coming over, he had also now just about managed to adjust his body-clock. He looked forward, though, to a short nap in the Mercedes on the way back to London and the British Museum; a nap en route, he assured us, should put him completely to rights.

'London and the British Museum'; the normal world seemed light-years away. And yet, through the latticed windows, dawn was spreading her pale fingers over the distant capital in what seemed a very normal fashion, and the new day was well on its way. Crow and I were now very tired, but such were those feelings of general well-being engendered by the protective proximity of the star-stones, that neither of us minded the heaviness of our bodies – at least we were completely clear-headed; our minds were free of morbid Cthonian undertones.

It was as I went into the galley to cook bacon and eggs for an early breakfast, as I passed down the short joining corridor between the bunkhouse and the galley proper, that I was thrown against the galley door when the houseboat suddenly rocked violently. From the bunkroom came the clatter of falling glasses, the thud of books, and Crow's startled query: 'What on earth . . . ?'

I opened the galley window and looked out on deck and across the river. The sun's edge was just showing above the horizon of trees and distant roofs. There was a very slight breeze up, but the river was white with mist.

Mentally echoing Titus Crow, I wondered: 'What on earth . . . ?' Had some lunatic gone up the river in a large motorboat at speed? But no, that could hardly be, I had heard no engine. In any case, it would have taken an ocean liner to create a wake like that! Even as these thoughts passed through my head *Seafree* keeled again, this time to an angle of about twenty degrees. Immediately, I found myself thinking of the Jordan document.

'De Marigny!' Crow's shout came from the open window even as I heard him skidding about on the momentarily sloping deck. 'Henri.' His feet clattered. 'Get that damned pistol of yours, quickly!' There was urgency in his voice, unnatural strain – and horror!

'No, no!' came the professor's shouted denial as the boat dipped and swayed. 'That's not the way, Crow. Silver bullets are no use against *this* thing!'

What thing?

I scrambled back through the galley door and down the corridor, across the bunkhouse floor, and up the three steps to the deck. There, clinging to the rail, their faces drawn and white, stood the two men. As the boat steadied itself, I joined them. 'What is it, Titus? What's wrong?'

'There's something out there, Henri, in the water. Something big! It just now made a rush at the boat – stopped about fifty feet short and sank down again into the water – a Sea-Shoggoth, I think, exactly like those dream-things I told you about.'

'Yes, a Sea-Shoggoth,' Peaslee breathed. 'One of the Deep Ones. All the way from Deep G'll-ho to the north,

154

I imagine. It can't harm us – ' He sounded sure enough of his facts, but nevertheless I noticed that his hushed voice trembled.

The mist was thick on the river, its milky tendrils and eddies coming almost up to the deck of the houseboat, making it seem as though we stood aboard a mere raft. I could hear the *chop* as the disturbed waters slapped the hull, but I could see nothing. I felt my pulse start to race and the short hairs prickling at the back of my neck. 'I'll get my pistol,' I said, intending to go back down into the boat.

As I turned from the rail Peaslee grabbed my arm. 'Useless, de Marigny,' he snapped. 'Pistols, no matter what kind of ammunition they take, are useless against this type of creature!'

'But where is the thing?' I asked, peering again at the misted waters.

As if in answer to my nervous question, indeed, as the last word left my lips, an iridescent, blackly shining column of what looked like mud or tar embedded with fragments of broken, multicoloured glass rose up out of the swirling river mist. Eight feet wide and all of twenty feet tall, dripping water and bobbing like some great sentient cork, the thing towered above the water . . . and the sun glinted from its surface and from its myriad eyes!

The creature – stank! There is simply no other way of expressing the nauseating stench that issued from it. Lines from Alhazred again leaped into my mind: 'By their smell shall ye know them,' and I knew exactly what the so-called 'mad' Arab had meant! It was the very smell of evil. Twice in a matter of hours my senses had been thus assaulted, and this time the worst! Thank the Lord that the houseboat was upwind, what little wind there was, of the horror; we received only a minimum, but even then too much, of that miasmal, deep-sea effluvium.

It had mouths, too, many of them, but I caught only a glimpse. As the thing made a frantic, nodding rush at the boat I threw myself down the steps after Kant's pistol. No matter what Peaslee said, I refused to stand undefended against *that*! Any weapon seemed better than none at all. In my panic I had completely forgotten the fact that we were not at all weaponless, that in fact we had the best possible protection! In any case, I couldn't find the pistol. Where had I put the thing?

The houseboat rocked again, yet more violently, and I scrambled back up the steps to the deck empty-handed. Fighting to keep his balance while hanging on to the rail with one hand, Peaslee was holding up a star-stone and shouting at the horror in the water. The thing was already rushing back in yet another monstrous, bobbing charge. My concentration divided itself equally between the professor and the creature bearing down upon the boat. Peaslee was rapidly chanting: 'Away, slime of the sea, back to your dark and pressured seat. With the authority of the Elder Gods themselves I command you. Away and leave us in peace!' The tremor had left his voice and his old, slim frame seemed somehow tall and powerful against the backdrop of iridescent horror sprouting beyond him from the river mist.

Before Peaslee's chanting and his showing of the star-stone there had been no sound from the Deep One other than the natural noise of the water rushing past its nightmare shape as it charged. Now –

It was screaming, apparently in rage and frustration, certainly in a manner suggesting some sort of alien mental agony. Its – voice? – had been just too far up the sonic scale before; there had been a high, almost inaudible whine in the air. Now, though, the professor's chanted words, repeated over and over again, were almost drowned out and I had to grit my teeth and slam my

156

hands to my ears as the creature lowered its hideous cries. Never before in my life had I heard so unbelievable a cacophony of incredible sounds all in one, and it was my fervent prayer that I never hear such sounds again!

The screaming was still in the main high-pitched, like a steam engine's whistle, but there were grunted under-tones, throbbing gasps or emissions such as the reptiles and great frogs make, impossible to put down on paper. Two more bobbing, water-spraying, abortive attempts it made to breach the invisible barrier between its awful body and the houseboat – and then it turned, sank, and finally left a thrashing, thinning wake in the rapidly clearing mist as it headed for London and the open sea beyond.

For a long time there was an awkward hush, wherein only the subsiding slap of wavelets against the hull, our erratic and harsh breathing, and the outraged cheeping of momentarily quieted birds disturbed the silence. Peaslee's voice, a little less steady now that it was all over, finally got through to me after a second asking of his question:

'How about breakfast, Henri? Won't it be spoiling?'

Crow laughed harshly as I explained that I had not yet managed to get breakfast started. He said: 'Breakfast? By God, Peaslee, but you won't catch me eating on this boat! I won't be here long enough – not now!'

'Perhaps you're right,' the professor hurriedly agreed. 'Yes, the sooner we get on our way, the better. We were perfectly safe, I assure you, but such things are always unnerving.'

'Unnerving!' *Ye Gods!*

It took us half an hour to get packed up; by 9:45 we were on our way in Crow's Mercedes.

We breakfasted at 10:30 in a pub on the approaches to the city proper. Guinness and ham sandwiches. We all were very hungry. As we finished off a second bottle each

(Peaslee's surprise at the black brew's pick-me-up quality was apparent) we also saw an end to our conversation regarding the morning's monstrous visitor.

Miskatonic and the Wilmarth Foundation, the professor declared, had long suspected a deep-sea citadel north of the British Isles, peopled by such creatures as only the Cthulhu Cycle of myth might spawn. They had good reasons for such suspicions; apparently G'll-ho was given mention in a fair number of the great works of named and anonymous occult authors. ('Occult' is a natural part of my vocabulary; I doubt if I shall ever learn how to leave it out of my life or thoughts, written or spoken.) Abdul Alhazred, in the *Necronomicon*, had named the place as 'Sunken G'lohee, in the Isles of Mist', and he had hinted that its denizens were the spawn of Cthulhu himself! More recently, Gordon Walmsley of Goole had recorded similar allusions in his alleged 'spoof' death-notes. Titus Crow, too, considering his dreams of a vast underwater fortress somewhere off the Vestmann Islands, where Surtsey belched forth in the agony of volcanic birth in 1963, concurred with the possibility of just such a submarine seat of suppurating evil.

Assuredly, the professor had it, the creature we had seen that morning had originated in G'll-ho. It had been sent, no doubt, on the telepathic instructions of Shudde-M'ell or his kind, to deliver the death-blow to two dangerous men. If Peaslee had not presented himself when he did . . . it did not bear thinking about.

While the professor's explanation regarding our visitor's origin seemed reasonably satisfactory to me, Crow was far from easy about it. Why then, he wanted to know, had similar beasts not been sent to deal with *Sea-Maid* when that rig had been drilling its inadvertently destructive bore off Hunterby Head? Again Peaslee had the answer to hand. Some of these horrors, he reminded us, were in direct opposition to one another – such as Cthulhu and Hastur. The type of creature as called up those cyclonic forces which sent *Sea-Maid* to the bottom, while it was not necessarily an enemy of the Lord of R'lyeh, was certainly inferior in the mythos; it was simply too lowly for Cthulhu, or any other of the greater powers of the CCD, to bother with. True, it had had the capacity to partly control the elements, and lesser creatures such as fishes, but the experience of the Wilmarth Foundation (which had dealt with such beings before) was that these were the least harmful of all the inmates of the Elder Gods' prisons.

The theory was, in fact, that such creatures were nothing more than low-order minions of the Great Ones proper, but that they had been imprisoned separately because of their huge size – in much the same way as large animals are kept in separate cages in zoos while smaller creatures are housed together. Certainly Shudde-M'ell had not been prisoned alone, as witness the G'harne eggs and the monstrous spread of the Cthonians through-out the world. Peaslee quite expected, before we were through with the Great Britain Project, that we should see an end put to any number of such beings. (Eventually, we were, in fact, witness to many such 'kills', and one which sticks in my mind quite vividly still, though I have at times tried to forget it. But I must keep that horror for later.)

The Deep Ones, though, quite apart from these appall-ing subterrene giants, came in a number of sorts and sizes. Their name, in fact, was a group heading, under which fell all manner of fishlike, protoplasmic, batrachian, and semi-human beings, united together in the worship of Dagon and the anticipated resurrection of Great Cthulhu. Neither Crow nor I was totally ignorant of these Deep Ones; we had both heard, over a period of time and from diverse sources, mad whispers echoing down the years of frightful occurrences at Innsmouth, a decaying seaport on the New England coast of America. Indeed, such was the macabre nature of the stories that leaked out of Innsmouth in the late 20s that certain of them, almost a decade later, were fictionalized in a number of popular fantastic magazines. The theme of these rumours (no longer rumours, for Peaslee assured us of their established *fact*; he positively asserted that Federal files were extant, copies of which had long been 'acquired' by the Wilmarth Foundation, which detailed the almost unbelievable occurrences of 1928) was that in the early 1800s certain traders of the old East-Indian and Pacific routes had had unsavoury dealings with degenerate Polynesian islanders. These natives had had their own 'gods', namely Cthulhu and Dagon (the latter having seen earlier worship by the Philistines and Phoenicians), and worshipped them in disgusting and barbaric ways. Eventually the New England sailors were inveigled into taking part in just such practices, apparently against the better judgement of many of them, and yet it seemed that the ways of the heathen Kanakas were not without their own doubtful rewards!

Innsmouth prospered, grew fat and rich as trade picked up, and soon strange gold changed hands in the streets of that doomed town. Esoteric churches opened – or rather temples – for purposes of even darker worship (the many seafarers had brought back strangely ichthyic Polynesian brides), and who could say how far things might have gone if, in 1927, the Federal Government had not been alerted to the growing menace?

In the winter of 1927–28, Federal agents moved in, and the end result was that half Innsmouth's inhabitants were banished (Peaslee had it that they had been sent off to scattered naval and military prisons and out-of-the-way asylums) and depth-charges were dropped off Devil's Reef in the Atlantic coast. There, in the untold depths of a natural rift, existed a weed-shrouded city of alien proportions and dimensions – Y'ha-nthlei – peopled by the Deep Ones, into which 'select' order many of the New England traders and their hideously blasphemous off-spring had been admitted since contact was first estab-lished with the Polynesians a century earlier. For those islanders of one hundred years gone had known far more than a close liaison with the Deep Ones of Polynesia – *and therefore so eventually did the New Englanders*.

The seafaring traders paid dearly for their adoption of the Kanaka 'faith' – and for less mentionable things – for by the time the Federal agents took control of Innsmouth hardly a single family existed in the town untainted by the shocking disfigurations of a stigma known locally as 'the Innsmouth Look'.

The Innsmouth Look! Frightful degenerations of mind and tissue . . . scaly skin, webbed fingers and toes . . . bulging fishlike eyes . . . *gills*!

And it was the Innsmouth Look that heralded the change from land-dweller to amphibian, from human to Deep One! Many of the town's inhabitants who escaped the horrified government agents did so by swimming out to Devil's Reef and diving down to Y'ha-nthlei, there to dwell with the Deep Ones proper, 'in wonder and glory for ever'.

These, then, were members of that seething submarine sect – but there were others.

There *were* others, more truly alien (Crow's 'survi-vors'), leftovers from an abyss of time and aeons before their aquatic phase, when the Earth knew the semiproto-plasmic tread of them and their masters and none other. It was one of these latter beings that had attempted the attack upon *Seafree* – which only Peaslee's star-stones and chantings had held at bay.

With all talk over, our meal done, and feeling the better for it, we left the pub and continued on our way. The journey was uneventful and quiet, with Crow driving while I relaxed in the back of the car. Beside me, Peaslee nodded and drowsed, no doubt making final subconscious adjustments to his body-clock.

That night, after the professor had paid a long, lone afternoon call to the British Museum, we all three congregated to sleep at Blowne House. For the first time in what seemed like years I slept peacefully, dreamlessly; so that not even certain vociferous trees in the garden, creaking through the dark hours, could disturb my·slumbers in any other than a tiny degree.

11

Horrors of Earth

(From de Marigny's Notebooks)

Many & multiform are ye dim horrors of Earth, infesting her
ways from ye very prime. They sleep beneath ye unturned stone;
they rise with ye tree from its root; they move beneath ye sea,
& in subterranean places they dwell in ye inmost adyta. Some
there are long known to man, & others as yet unknown, abiding
ye terrible latter days of their revealing. Those which are ye
most dreadful & ye loathliest of all are haply still to be declared.

Abdul Alhazred: Feery's
Notes on the Necronomicon.

Some months have passed; they seem like years. Certainly I have aged years. Many of the things I have seen
have proved almost too much to believe – too fantastic
even to retain – and, indeed, I actually find the pictures
fading from my memory. As the days go by, I have more
and more trouble focusing my mind upon any set instance,
any individual incident; and yet, paradoxically, it is
undeniable that certain things have left livid scars upon
the surface of my mind.

Perhaps this reluctance of mine to remember is simply
a healing process, and who can say but that when I have
'healed' completely the entire episode might well have
vanished for ever from my memory?

It is because of this – because there is a very real chance
of my 'forgetting' all that has gone since the advent of
Professor Wingate Peaslee of Miskatonic – that now,
without any conscious attempt to stress the horror in any
way, in an earnest effort to get the thing down as
unemotionally as possible, I make the following entries in
my notebook.

Possibly my *rejection* began before Peaslee and the subsequent horrors, for I find that those monstrous occurrences aboard *Seafree* before his coming are also dimming in my mind's eye, and to recall them in any sort of detail I find it necessary to resort to a reading of my earlier notebooks. Yet this, surely, is a mercy. Who was it said that the most merciful thing in the world is the inability of the human mind to correlate all its contents? And yet, if only to retain the following as an *account* as opposed to a memory, I find that I must now correlate at least certain occurrences . . .

It was late August. The three of us, myself, Crow, and Peaslee, were looking down from a low bramble- and gorse-girt hill across an area of wild open moorland. Of course, it is not my intention to divulge our exact whereabouts as they were, but we were well 'out-of-the-way'. Three weed-grown and neglect-obscured tracks led out of the area, and each of them, from a distance some four miles out from the hub of the operation, carried warning notices such as: *Danger, Unexploded Bombs,* and *Government Property, Keep Out,* or *Tank Range, Firing in Progress!* Such notices had had Crow somewhat perturbed for a time, until Peaslee reminded him of the Wilmarth Foundation's influence in high places – even in certain governmental circles! To reinforce the posted warnings a number of Foundation men with guard dogs prowled the perimeter of the area. It would be disastrous to allow the leak of any untoward tales into the mundane world outside.

No more than a mile away, and in a central, strangely barren area, the superstructure of a great drilling-rig towered up to clear but grey skies. Beneath that threatening pylon of girders and gears, fourteen hundred feet down in the bedrock, one of those monsters met before by Pongo Jordan and his ill-fated rig *Sea-Maid* slumbered in its ancient prison. That the Cthonian was in fact prisoned had long been ascertained; the telepath who first tracked the thing down had recognized well-known mind-patterns and had picked up mental impressions implying great size. It was indeed one of those outsize, low-order minions of the Old Ones which, in Peaslee's own words, 'were the least harmful of all the inmates of the Elder Gods' prisons.'

Despite a warm sun the afternoon breeze, seeming to spring from somewhere down in the direction of the drilling-rig, was surprisingly chill. We had the collars of our coats turned up against it. Peaslee was in walkie-talkie contact with a British telepath, Gordon Finch, whose mental images – relayed to us as he received them and as the climax drew to a close – came over the air loud and clear. The huge Cthonian (possibly undisturbed for millennia) had started to emerge from its comalike slumbers some hours before and was now becoming more alert, its monstrous mind forming rather clearer pictures for Finch to 'tune in' on. Crow, powerful binoculars about his neck, peered intently into lenses sighted on the matchstick people and Dinky-Toy vehicles moving about down in the distant spider web of paths and tracks cut through the greyly withered gorse and heather.

A Land Rover, churning sand and browned gorse flowers, issued blue exhaust smoke as it powered through dry, scanty foliage at the foot of our hill. The bright yellow bandanna of the driver identified him as Bernard 'Pongo' Jordan himself. He was on his way up to our vantage point, from which he hoped to photograph the kill. This in no way reflected a morbid 'thing' of Pongo's, on the contrary, for any and all information on the CCD was of the utmost importance to the Wilmarth Foundation. After death most of the Cthonians rotted so fast that identification of their matter was literally impossible – and very few of the various species had anything even remotely approaching similarities of makeup! Even the count of the heartbeat – or the beat of whatever organ the creature possessed which might stand for a heart – would prove of value; and it was that chiefly, the gory spurt of alien juices, that Pongo intended to film.

In a matter of minutes the Rover had bumped its way up to the crest upon which we stood. Pongo slewed the vehicle about and parked it none too carefully beside Crow's big black Mercedes. Before the motor coughed itself out the huge Yorkshireman had joined us. He pulled a hip-flask from the pocket of his denim jacket and took a deep draught before offering the whisky to Crow, who declined with a smile.

'No thanks, Pongo – I prefer brandy. We have a flask in the car.'

'You, de Marigny?' The big man's voice, despite its roughness, was tense, nervous.

'Thanks, yes.' I took the flask from him. I hardly needed the drink really, but Jordan's jumpiness was infectious. And little wonder, for there was something . . . wrong . . . somewhere. We could all sense it, a disturbing feeling of impending, well, *something* in the air. The lull before a storm.

Gordon Finch's voice came louder now, clearer over the walkie-talkie, which Peaslee had turned up full volume for our benefit.

'The thing's not quite fully aware yet, it's still half asleep, but it knows something's up. I'm going to go deeper into its mind, see what I can see.'

'Careful, Finch,' Peaslee said quickly into his handset. 'Don't alert the creature whatever you do. We can never be certain – we don't know what it's capable of.'

For perhaps half a minute there was an almost audible

silence from the walkie-talkie. Then, simultaneous with
Jordan's reminder that there were only six minutes left to
penetration, Finch's voice, ethereal now as his mind
entered deeper into the Cthonian's miasmal mentality,
sounded again from Peaslee's handset:

'It's . . . *strange!* Strangest sensations I've ever known.
There's pressure, the weight of countless tons of . . .
rock.' The voice trailed off.

Peaslee waited a second, then snapped: 'Finch, get a
grip on yourself, man! What's wrong?'

'Eh?' I could almost see the telepath shaking himself.
Now his voice was eager: 'Nothing's wrong, Professor,
but I want to go deeper. I believe I can get *right inside*
this one!'

'I forbid it – ' Peaslee railed.

'Never forbid an Englishman anything.' Finch's voice
hardened. 'A few more minutes and the thing'll be
finished, gone for ever – and it's millions of years old. I
want . . . I want to *know!*'

Again the silence from the handset, while Peaslee grew
more agitated by the second. Then –

'Pressure . . .' The voice was fainter, trancelike. 'Tons
and tons of crushing . . . weight.'

'Where is he down there?' Crow asked sharply, never
for a second taking the binoculars from his eyes.

'In the control shack by the rig,' Jordan answered, his
camera starting to whir in his hands. 'The others should
be clearing out now, moving back – all bar the lads on the
rig itself – and Finch should get out too. He'll get
drenched in muck when she goes through; and when they
shoot off the bomb – ' He left his thoughts unspoken.

By 'the bomb' I knew he meant the explosive harpoon
set in the head of the great drill. As soon as the bit went
through into the softer *stuff* of the Cthonian, the bomb
would automatically fire, shooting itself deep into the guts

167

of the monster before exploding. Finch was supposed to break contact with the creature's thoughts before then.

'Four minutes,' Pongo said.

'*Trapped!*' came Finch's voice again. '*Trapped down . . . HERE! Nothing has changed – but why do I wake? I have only to flex the muscles of my body, arch my back to break out, to be free to go – as I went free so long ago – in search of the little creatures – to slake this great thirst with their red –*

'*Ahhh! I can see the little ones in my mind as I remember them, when once before, following the great roaring and crushing and shifting of the earth, I went free! With their little arms, hairy bodies, and futile clubs. I remember their screams as I absorbed them into myself.*

'*But I dare not, CANNOT, break free! Despite my strength, a greater power holds me, the mind-chains of THEM and their barriers – the Great Elder Gods who prisoned me so long, long ago – who returned to prison me again after but a brief freedom when the earth tore itself and their sigils were scattered.*

'*I am STILL prisoned, and more, there is . . . danger!*'

'Finch, come out of there!' Peaslee yelled frantically into his handset. 'Let the thing be, man, and get out!'

'*DANGER!*' Finch's now alien voice continued, coarse and slurred. '*I can sense . . . little ones! Many of them . . . above me . . . and something approaches!*'

'Just over two minutes!' Jordan blurted, his voice cracking.

Now there was only a harsh gasping from the walkie-talkie, and above it Crow's sudden, amazed exclamation: 'Why, *I* can feel the thing, too! It's sending out mind-feelers. It knows what we're up to. It's more intelligent than we thought, Peaslee, superior to any of the others we've so far done away with.' He let his binoculars dangle and put his hands up to his ears, as if to shut out some dreadful sound. His eyes closed and his face screwed up in pain. 'The thing's frightened – no, *angry*! My God!'

'*I am not defenceless, little ones!*' Finch's horribly altered voice screamed from the handset. '*Trapped, true, but NOT defenceless. You have learned much in the passage of time – but I, too, have powers! I can't stop that which you send burrowing down towards me, but I have . . . powers!*'

Crow screamed harshly and fell to his knees, rocking to and fro and clutching madly at his head. At that moment I was very glad that my own psychic or telepathic talents were as yet undeveloped!

'The sky!' Peaslee gasped, turning my attention from the now prostrate Titus Crow. 'Look at the sky!'

Black clouds boiled and tossed where only grey skies had opened scant moments before, and lightning played high in the cauldron of suddenly rushing air. In another second a great wind sprang up, whipping our coats about us and snatching at Jordan's yellow bandanna. Down in the depression gorse bushes came loose from the sandy earth to swirl into the air as if at the mercy of a whole nest of dust devils.

'Get down!' Jordan yelled, his voice barely audible over the wild rush of wind, flying sand and bits of gorse, heather and bracken. 'There's little over a minute to go – down for your lives!'

We all fell to the ground immediately. Crow now lay there quite still. I grabbed at thick heather roots and flung an arm about my friend's motionless body. The wind was icy now, seeming to rush up at us from the rig, and angry thunder boomed while flashes of lightning lit up the sky, etching in outlines of jet the rig's distant structure upon the gaunt backdrop of moor and low bleak hills.

Screams had begun to echo up from the declivity, barely heard over the mad, pandemoniac roar of tortured air and sky, causing me to reach through suddenly slashing rain for Crow's binoculars. I freed them from his neck and held them to my face, drawing the structures in the declivity closer with quick, jerky movements of my trembling hands.

'*The thing in the ground comes closer,*' screamed Finch's voice (or was it Finch's voice?) from Peaslee's handset. '*And I sense its nature. So be it! I die – but first feel the might of (. . . ?) and his wrath, and let my arms reach out for the surface that my mouths might drink one last time! Now know the LUST of (. . . ?), little ones, and his power over the very elements! Remember and tremble when the stars are right and Great Lord Cthulhu comes again!*'

I had finally managed to focus the binoculars on the rig and the small shacks surrounding it. In one of those buildings the telepath Finch sat, his mind still in contact with that of the great beast down in the bowels of the earth. I shuddered uncontrollably as I pictured the man down there.

Lorries and smaller vehicles were now moving away from the perimeter of the work area, and running figures, fighting the buffeting wind and squalling rain on foot. Then came horror!

Even as I watched, the lightning began to flash with more purpose, great bolts striking down accurately at the rig and its appurtenances. Running figures burst into electric flame and crumpled while lorries and Land Rovers, careening madly about, roared up in gouting fire and ruin. Girders melted and fell from the now blazing rig, and great patches of the scant vegetation surrounding that structure hissed and steamed before crackling into red and orange death.

'Time's up,' yelled Jordan in my ear; 'the bomb should fire any second now. That ought to put a stop to the bastard's game!'

Even as the Yorkshireman yelled the voice of the thing that had been 'Gordon Finch screamed from Peaslee's handset:

'*I am STRICKEN! – Na-ngh . . . ngh . . . ngh-ya – Great Ubbo-sathla, your child dies – but give me now strength for a final drinking – let me stretch myself this one last time – DEFY the sigils of the Elder Gods – na-argh . . . ngh . . . ngh! – Arghhh-k-k-k! – Hyuh, yuh, h-yuh-yuh!*'

As these monstrous, utterly abhuman exhortations and syllables crackled in hideously distorted cacophony from the walkie-talkie, so I witnessed the final abomination.

Dimly I was aware of Peaslee's incoherent cry as the very ground beneath us jounced and slipped; in the corner of my consciousness I knew that Jordan had attempted to get to his feet, only to be thrown down again by the dancing ground – but mainly my eyes and mind were riveted on the nightmare scene afforded me by Crow's accursed binoculars, those glasses that my nerveless fingers could not put down!

For down in the valley depression great rifts had appeared in the earth – and from these seismic chasms terrible tendrils of grey, living matter spewed forth in awful animation!

Flailing spastically – like great, mortally wounded snakes across the battered, blistered terrain – the tendrils moved, and soon some of them encountered the fleeing men! Great crimson maws opened in grey tendril ends, and –

Finally I managed to hurl the binoculars away. I closed my eyes and pressed my face down into the wet grass and sand. In that same instant there came a tremendous crack of lightning, the incredible flickering brightness of which I could sense even with my eyes closed and covered, and immediately there followed such an explosion and a rushing, reeking *stench* as to make my very senses temporarily depart . . .

I do not know how long it was before I felt Jordan's hand upon my shoulder or heard his voice inquiring as to my condition, but when next I lifted my head the sky was clear once again and a freshening breeze blew over the blasted hill. Peaslee was sitting up, silently shaking his head from side to side and gazing down at the scene below. I followed his gaze.

Fires still raged down there, emitting columns of blue smoke among the shrivelled gorse bushes and brittle heather. The rig was a twisted mass of blackened metal, fallen on its side. One or two scorched trucks still moved, making their way tiredly towards our hill, and a handful of tattered figures stumbled dazedly about. Moans and cries for help drifted up to us. Grey, vile ichor steamed and bubbled in liquid catabolism, filling the newly opened cracks in the earth like pus in hellish sores.

'We have to help them,' Jordan said simply. I nodded and climbed weakly to my feet. Peaslee, too, stood up. Then, remembering, I got down on one knee and gently shook Titus Crow's shoulder. He came to a moment later, but was incapable of aiding us in the work we now had to do; his mental encounter, though brief, had been too shattering.

As the three of us walked towards Jordan's Rover, I picked up the walkie-talkie from where Peaslee had left it. In a moment of thoughtlessness I turned up the volume – and understood why the professor had left the handset behind. There were . . . *noises*: low, incoherent mouthings, snatches of childish song, giggles of imbecile laughter . . .

* * *

We lost six dead, five missing – and one, poor Finch, hopelessly insane. There were injuries, but in the main these were minor: burns, cuts, and bruises. The fact that another Cthonian – one of the 'least harmful of all' the subterrene species – was dead seemed hardly ample justification for such losses. Still, these were the first casualties the Foundation had suffered in the whole Great Britain Project to date.

The newspapers the next day were full of the earth tremors that had rocked the entire Northeast seaboard – to a lesser degree the titanic blast of ignited gases 'inadvertently released from beneath the surface of the earth by members of a scientific drilling project'. Too, ground rumblings had been heard and felt in the Cotswolds, and Surtsey had flared briefly forth again to send up clouds of volcanic steam. Freak storms vied for space with these items in the press: hailstones as big as golf balls in the South; freak lightning over many parts of England, particularly Durham and Northumberland; lashing, incessant rain the whole afternoon in the West. Lunatic asylums had also been affected, alarmingly so, by the Wilmarth Foundation's machineries that day. Reports of uprisings, mass rebellions, and escapes were legion. 'Moon, tide, and weather cycles', alienists and psychologists vaguely had it . . .

Of the form, type and characteristics of the Cthonian we destroyed that day little yet is known. That it was 'a child of Ubbo-sathla' seems as much as we are ever likely to learn. Within hours of the final explosion of its body-gases (gases which must have been closely related to methane, and under pressure at that), its tendril-substances – indeed, so far as is known, its entire body – had rotted and disappeared. Subsequent soundings of the space it had occupied underground have shown that the thing was almost *a quarter of a mile long and a third that distance across!*

We do not even positively know what the creature's name was. We heard it spoken, certainly, by Finch in his telepathic trance, but such was its sound and the arrangements of its consonants that human vocal cords cannot emulate them. Only a man in actual mind-contact with such a being, as poor Gordon Finch was, might be able to approximate such intricacies. The nearest we can get to it in written English is: Cgfthgnm'o'th.

Regarding that forebear mentioned by the Cthonian in its death agonies: it would appear that Ubbo-sathla (Ubho-Shatla, Hboshat, Bothshash, etc.) was here even before Cthulhu and his spawn first seeped down from the stars; that (if we can take Finch's mind-interpretations as a true translation), Ubbo-sathla was drawn into kinship with Cthulhu after the latter's domination of pre-Earth. These conclusions, such as they are, seem borne out by the following fragment from the disturbing *Book of Eibon*:

. . . For Ubbo-sathla is the source and the end. Before the coming of Zhothaquah or Yok-Zothoth or Kthulhut from the stars, Ubbo-sathla dwelt in the steaming fens of the new-made Earth: a mass without head or members, spawning the grey, formless efts of the prime and the grisly prototypes of terrene life . . . And all earthy life, it is told, shall go back at last through the great cycle of time to Ubbo-sathla . . .

It took a fortnight to clear up the mess, physical and administrational, and to cover our tracks – not to mention another week of fast talking in high places by Peaslee and other senior American members – before the operations of the Wilmarth Foundation in the British Isles could continue. In the end, though, the long-laid plans went ahead.

12
Familiarity Breeds
(From de Marigny's Notebooks)

On this occasion, some weeks gone, Crow and I were travelling in the Mercedes down from the Northwest. A few days earlier, in the Scottish Southern Uplands, the Wilmarth Foundation had forced a Cthonian – one of the last of the static or prisoned forms 'indigenous' to Great Britain and her waters – from its burrow deep beneath a mountain cleft. The being, a small one of its kind, had then been hosed down (literally hosed down *to nothing!*) with powerful jets of water. This had been at a place central in the Uplands; a sparse, very underpopulated area between Lanark and Dumfriesshire. The sight of the creature's violent thrashing as it melted beneath the sustained jets of lethal water, until finally it lay inert, a pool of awful, semiorganic putrescence bubbling off in vile evaporation, was one which had seared itself upon the retina of my very being. I was in fact still seeing the awful thing in my mind's eye as Crow drove the car south away from the scene of the 'kill'.

Following this latest offensive, Peaslee had flown from Glasgow to London to meet friends and colleagues coming in from America. These Americans were bringing freshly devised seismological equipment with which they hoped to follow the tracks of Shudde-M'ell's mobile Cthonian 'hordes' if the remainder of that species in Britain should make a dash for it, as certain of the Foundation's telepaths seemed to suspect they might. Of late the latter subterrene group, nests and individual members alike, had apparently developed a means of shielding their minds (and therefore their presence or whereabouts) from all but the most powerful of the telepaths. Crow's limited telepathic power, following the horror of the moor, had seemed to leave him. He was, though, he had assured me privately, otherwise as 'physically aware' as ever.

It was about noon. We were, I remember, passing through a lonely region some miles to the east of Penrith. For quite some time Titus Crow had driven in what I had taken to be silent thoughtfulness. At the very edge of my consciousness, I had been taking in something of the terrain through which the big car passed. Automatically, as is sometimes its wont, my mind had partly separated its attentions – between monstrous memories of the dissolving horror in the hills and, as I have said, the country through which we passed – when suddenly, for no apparent reason, I found myself filled with an as yet obscure inner concern.

The area was bleak. A steep and rocky hillside tilted jaggedly to the right of the road, fell abruptly away to the left. The road itself was narrow and poorly surfaced, faintly misted in front and behind, and the mist was thickening as it rolled down off the hills marching away southward.

I had just noticed the peculiarly ominous aspect of the place when it dawned on me that I had a headache, something I had not known for months, since first Peaslee joined us from America. The recognition of this fact came hand in hand with the abrupt, shocking memory of the professor's warning: 'Always remember – they *never* stop trying! You must carry these things wherever you go from now on, *but even so you must try not to venture anywhere below the surrounding ground-level. I mean that you're to keep out of valleys, gullies, quarries, mines, subways, and so on. They can get at you indirectly – a sudden earthquake, a fall of rock . . .*'

'Titus!' I gasped out loud. 'Titus, where the hell are you going? We're not on the route we intended to take. We ought to have turned *across* country miles back, following the A-Sixty-Nine to the Northeast coast as we planned!' I gazed fearfully out of my window at the steep declivity falling away, and on the other side of the car, the now almost vertical wall of rock reaching up into misty heights.

Crow had jumped nervously as I commenced my outburst, and now he applied the brakes and brought the car to a halt. He shook his head, dazedly rubbing at his eyes. 'Of course we should have followed the A-Sixty-Nine,' he eventually agreed, frowning in concern. Then: '*What on earth . . . ?*' His eyes lit feverishly, strange understanding, horrible recognition showing in them.

'De Marigny – I think I understand why the Foundation has recently been plagued with an inordinately high percentage of freak "accidents", suicides, and deaths. I think I understand, *and I think that we're the next on the list!*'

No sooner had he spoken when, with a suddenness that caused the hair of my head to stand up straight and the shorter hairs of my neck to bristle and prickle, the ground beneath our stationary vehicle trembled; the rumble was audible even over the noise of the idling engine!

The next instant, I admit it, I screamed aloud; but Crow was already in action, releasing the handbrake, revving the engine, throwing the car into reverse gear. Nor were his instantaneous reactions any too soon. Even as the car lurched backwards on spinning wheels a great boulder, followed by smaller rocks, pebbles, and tons of earth, smashed down from above on to the road where the Mercedes had been but a moment earlier. At the same time, too, we heard (with our minds if not actually

177

with our ears) the morbid, alien dronings of an all too recognizable chant:

> Ce'haiie ep-ngh fl'hur G'harne fhtagn,
> Ce'haiie fhtagn ngh Shudde-M'ell.

'Nowhere to turn,' Crow gasped, still reversing, 'but if I can back her up far enough – '

Shattering his hopes and the unspoken prayers of both of us, the mist, as if answering some hellish call (which I can readily believe it was), fell in opaque and undulating density all about us.

'My God!' I gasped, as again Crow brought the car to a halt.

'Can't see a thing,' my friend shouted, his face grey now as the surrounding wall of ghostly gloom without. 'You'll have to get out, de Marigny, and quickly! The windows have misted over completely. Put your hand in the centre of the rear window, and walk down the middle of the road until you find a spot where I can turn the car around. Can you do it?'

'I'll damned well try,' I croaked, my mouth dry with nameless fear.

'You'll need do more than try,' he grimly told me as I opened the door. 'If not . . . we're done for!'

I slammed the door behind me, ran around to the back of the car, and pressed my right palm to the damp glass of the rear window. The engine roared and Crow's shout came to me from his open window: 'Good, Henri – now walk up the road, or better still sit on the boot, and guide me by moving your hand left or right as the road bends. Good, that's it, we're off!'

I continued as I had been instructed, sitting on the boot and moving my hand behind me over the glass of the window, directing Crow as he reversed the big car carefully along the mist-shrouded, narrow road. On three or four separate occasions rocks tumbled down from above, dislodged from the unseen heights by continued subterranean tremblings; and all the while I could sense, at the back of my mind, *Their* awful, droning chanting!

After what seemed like several ages the mist seemed to lift a little, the road widened, and there appeared a shallow, weed-choked reentry in the cliff-face just wide enough to accommodate the car. With a warning cry to Crow, I slid from the boot, ran around to the front, and directed him as he began to swing the rear end of the Mercedes off the road and into the cleft.

At this point I came very close to disaster. For suddenly, without any sort of warning, there came a low rumble from deep in the ground and the whole section of road where I stood jerked and shook violently. I was pitched backwards, off balance, over the edge of the road and head-over-heels down the steep decline beyond. Fortunately I did not fall far, no more than twelve feet or so, but I landed jarringly on my shoulder. Dazedly I struggled to my feet. I was on a wide natural ledge, beyond which the ground fell away and down to the unseen valley below. Again the mist had thickened and now there was a perceptible and rapidly increasing aura of dread and hideous expectancy in the damp air.

'Crow!' I yelled, trying vainly to scramble up the steep incline to the road. 'Titus, where are you?'

The next instant I was faced with something so monstrously terrifying that for a moment I thought my heart must stop. To my left, at a distance of no more than fifteen feet, the very limit of my vision in the mist, the face of the pebbly incline *burst outward* in a shower of stones and earth – and then –

– *Horror!*

I backed away, unashamedly babbling, screaming

Crow's name repeatedly as the – *Thing* – came after me. It was octopoid, this dweller in the earth . . . flowing tentacles and a pulpy grey-black, elongated sack of a body . . . rubbery . . . exuding a vilely stinking whitish slime . . . eyeless . . . headless, too . . . Indeed, I could see no distinguishing features at all other than the reaching, groping tentacles. Or was there – yes! – a *lump* in the upper body of the thing . . . a container of sorts for the brain, or ganglia, or whichever diseased organ governed this horror's loathsome life!

But it was closer, this spawn of Shudde-M'ell, it was almost upon me! I felt somehow rooted to the spot – fixed immobile, as if my feet were stuck in mental molasses, a fly in the ointment of the Cthonian group-mind – hearing the dreadful droning chant, my eyes wide open and popping and my mouth slack, my hair standing straight up on my head . . .

My star-stone!

Automatically, through all the shattering terror of my fear, I found myself reaching for that talisman of the Elder Gods – *but my jacket, with the star-stone safe in the inside pocket, was still in the Mercedes where I had left it.*

I was conscious of the ground beneath the pulpy horror before me *flowing* like water, flowing and steaming in the heat that the hellish Cthonian generated, and of those areas of the creature's body that touched the ground glowing and changing colour constantly. My God! It was upon me! Tentacles reached . . .

'*De Marigny!*' It was Crow's voice, and even as I heard his cry through the hypnotic chanting and the high-pitched screaming (which I hardly recognized as my own), even as his shout came to me, a star-stone – my own or Crow's, I didn't care – fell from above directly in the path of the looming star-spawn . . .

The effect was immediate and definite. The huge, alien

slug of a being before me reared back and almost toppled from the ledge; the mind-chants turned instantaneously to mental mewlings and gibberings with overtones of the utmost fear, and with incredible agility the thing finally turned in its slimy tracks to slither and flop away from me along the ledge. At what it must have taken to be a safe distance, with its tentacles whipping in a fearsome rage, the Cthonian turned in towards the cliff-face and moved forward, passing *into* the wall of earth and rock. For a few moments liquid earth and stone flowed like water from the hole the being left, then that part of the steep incline collapsed and I was left with only the abominable smell of the thing.

It was then I realized that I was still down on my knees with my hands held out before me; I had frozen in that position when it seemed certain that the Cthonian must take me. At the same time, too, I heard Crow's voice again, calling me from above. I glanced up. My friend was flat on the road, his face white and staring, his arms outstretched with my jacket dangling from his hands.

'Quickly, Henri, for God's sake! Quickly, before they have time to reorganize!'

I got to my feet, snatched up the precious star-stone, and put it in my trouser pocket, then caught hold of the dangling jacket and scrambled frantically, with Crow's assistance, to the tarmac surface of the road above. I saw that Crow had managed to get the car turned about, and breathed a sigh of relief as I slipped into the front passenger seat.

The ground trembled again as Titus put the car into gear, but a second later we were away, tyres screaming and lights cutting the curtain of mist like a knife. 'A close one, de Marigny,' my friend offered.

'Close! By God – I never want it any closer!' I told him.
Half a mile later there was no trace of the mist, and

wherever it had gone my headache had gone with it. Once more under control, I asked Crow what he had meant earlier when he mentioned the Foundation's recent plague of accidents, suicides, and deaths

'Yes,' he answered. 'Well, you remember how of late our telepaths have been having difficulty contacting the Cthonians; I think I can guess what those monsters have been up to. It dawned on me back there when first we realized something was wrong. I think that the burrowers have been concentrating their powers, massing their minds, overcoming the protective powers of the star-stones to a degree and *getting through* to Foundation members – just as today they got through to us. They've been dealing with us one at a time, which would explain our recent losses. It's no coincidence, de Marigny, that those losses have been such as defy any sort of accounting, and it's this new ability of theirs to get through to us that's deadened the Foundation's awareness of what's been going on! The sooner we let Peaslee and the others know, the better.' He put his foot down on the accelerator and the car sped us safely on our way.

13

The Very Worm That Gnaws

(From de Marigny's Diary)

The threat posed by the Cthonian ability to get at us in
mass mental-sendings is at an end; a special delivery of a
great number of star-stones from the United States has
seen to that. Also (and as our telepaths have suspected
for some time), the remaining Cthonians are attempting a
sort of exodus back to Africa; indeed, they have already
commenced the move. It was a nest of them, on their way
down- and across-country to the coast, that waylaid Crow
and me in that hill pass. They had obviously massed their
minds against the two of us – perhaps helped by others of
their shuddersome species, possibly even Shudde-M'ell
himself, wherever he might be – and unbeknown to us,
having overcome the shielding powers of our star-stones,
they had thus learned of our plans to drive south to
Dover. After that, it had only remained for them to make
a special mental effort to lead us away from the route we
had intended to take, and then intercept and ambush our
car at a favourable spot. We had been meant to die in
that initial avalanche of dislodged earth and boulders.
The plan had gone astray and they had been forced to try
other methods. Overcoming the power of the star-stones
in a direct confrontation, however, had proved a far
different kettle of fish to doing it en masse and at a
distance; and there they failed, when, as it has been seen,
the sigil of the Elder Gods had the final say. They had
doubtless been members of the same nest (the barest
nucleus of a nest, thank God, and comparatively young
ones at that) that Williams the telepath reported when

first he quartered Scotland from his plane; the nest that subsequently seemed to disappear into thin air – or earth, as the case is. We have two telepaths tracking them even now as they burrow in the deep earth.

10th Oct.

Peaslee caught a man last night trying to break into his hotel room in London, where he has set up his HQ. He threatened the intruder with a pistol, whereupon the fellow started to froth at the mouth and threw himself over the balcony rail. Peaslee's quarters are on the fifth floor! The professor escaped involvement in the subsequent police investigations.

11th Oct.

Jordan has quickly set up his wells in the now familiar pattern at a spot not far out of Nottingham. He hopes to catch the nest of nightmares Crow and I had dealings with in the hills up north. We are lucky in that the site is an old extensive army barracks complex – 'Government Property' – and that the whole area for half a mile around is Out-of-Bounds to the general public, as it is being demolished. The place is scheduled for redevelopment; possibly the construction of a power-station. I have a feeling it's just as well the place is coming down – particularly if what has happened at some of the other star-well sites should happen there.

13th Oct.

Regarding the exodus of the Cthonians: the British Isles are obviously too restricting for the horrors. What with Peaslee and the Wilmarth Foundation – why, the beings are no less prisoned now than were their prime forebears millennia ago in Dead G'harne; for here they are being slowly but surely tracked down and destroyed! If those of them that remain – damn few now – can make it back to Africa they stand a good chance of losing themselves completely in that vast continent, later to begin the insidious threat elsewhere. Many of them have already made the crossing beneath the Channel, but that hardly means that they've escaped. The Frenchies are doing their bit. The Foundation has men in France, and Peaslee has very big friends in power over there. He gets a lot of confidential letters with the Bibliothèque Nationale postmark.

There are still a number of the burrowers here in England, though, and during the last few days there have been tremors and minor subsidences all down the country, converging into three definite tracks towards Tenterden. Looking back I see that it was a week ago, on the sixth, that the Foundation trapped and exterminated no less than a dozen of the horrors on Salisbury Plain; and already, of the prisoned, 'harmless' species, these islands have just about been cleansed.

16th Oct.

The last few weeks have seen a number of arrests by Foundation members of so-called 'suspicious persons'. Usually these arrests have been made in areas directly occupied by the members concerned, often on actual star-well sites or in other planned locations. There was that one Peaslee got on the tenth, and two others were picked up in the barracks complex in Notts. Invariably persons thus arrested try to escape, but just as surely if they fail or if they are caught a second time they become instantly bereft of mind and will: the burrowers beneath have no time for failures! For these people are of course under the influence of the CCD – unsound men and women, usually of frail bodies and even frailer minds – but these last few days the numbers of such incidents have seen a sharp decline.

The insidious, crawling inundation of the British Isles by Shudde-M'ell's kin is at an end. Jordan's wells in their Nottinghamshire locations are being dismantled. That last nest must have got wind of our plans. It made no difference, however, and the end result was the same. They were picked up by a telepath as they made a panic-dash out from Bridlington under the North-Sea. They could hardly have chosen a worse route from their own point of view. There is a deep rift, a fault in the submarine strata, fifteen miles out from Bridlington. Our guess was that the horrors would not be too deep in the rocks when they passed beneath the fault. With the Royal Navy's assistance – ostensibly the command ship and its two submarine subordinates were on 'manoeuvres' – the place was quickly rigged with very powerful depth-charges; on this occasion there was no trouble from the Deep Ones in any form. At 3:30 this morning, on the instructions of Hank Silberhutte (one of the best of the American telepaths), the bombs were set off by radio signal from a fishing vessel out of Hull. Silberhutte reports complete success! The Admiralty, as a cover against any leakage of the facts, will put out a press item tomorrow on the supposed discovery of a sunken German World War II warship and the destruction of its huge and dangerously explosive cargo by depth-charge. It would appear that the arms of the Wilmarth Foundation continue to be far-reaching!

23rd Oct.

So far as is known not a single member of any of the diverse Cthonian species remains as a potential horror within Great Britain or her territorial waters. They have all been either destroyed or chased out. From the beginning there have been confusion reports from a number of our telepaths on impressions they seemed to be getting from a certain area deep beneath the Yorkshire Moors; but these 'reflections', as the telepaths term such false impressions, have now been discounted. Certainly there is nothing down there of the Cthonians as we have come to know them.

Here, however, a note of unique interest – 'Nessie' is a plesiosaur! Scotland has the world's last prehistoric monsters; five of them in fact, two adults and three young ones. A final telepathic check of the entire landmass, from John o'Groats to Land's End, brought this information to light. Nothing malignant in Loch Ness, on the contrary, but nevertheless the telepaths did pick up the weak, placidly watery thoughts of Earth's last dinosaurs. God! What wouldn't I give to be able to break the news to the press . . . ?

28th Oct.

Vive la France! I'm proud to be called de Marigny! Three underground atomic tests in the Algerian Desert in the last twenty-four hours! A few more of the damned horrors that won't be making it home.

30th Nov.

Word has just come in from Peaslee, now back at Miskatonic, that those phases of the American Project which were carried out simultaneously with certain of the major operations in Great Britain were more than moderately successful. It must be admitted, though, that in the United States and South America the task is far greater and the horrors apparently far more diverse and not confined alone to subterranean planes of existence. Certain wooded and mountainous regions (chiefly the Catskills, the Adirondacks, and the Rockies), the Great Lakes and other, more remote or obscure stretches of water; vast areas in and about New England, Wisconsin, Vermont, Oklahoma, and the Gulf of Mexico; and a dozen other places along the Andes in South America (there'll be trouble there), are all scheduled for the most minute mental and physical investigation and eventual 'pest control', to put it in the professor's own words.

And yet Peaslee's report is encouraging, for it appears that the incidence of free, mobile agencies is less in proportion to what it was here in England. The Americas do have a big problem, though, in the numbers of humans (and in some cases, particularly in New England, *semi-humans*) 'in Their employ!' Again, as in 1928, special agents are infiltrating certain of the backwater seaports on the New England coast.

6th Dec.

Cthulhu strikes back! Angered beyond endurance (Peaslee has it), Cthulhu has finally lashed out, proving once and for all his definite continued existence and potency here and now on Earth. How the Foundation and its many worldwide departments have managed to cover it all up – what chains they've put on the free world's presses – I don't suppose I shall ever learn.

Alerted by powerful telepathic currents emanating from somewhere in the Pacific, five Foundation telepaths – receptive where others mercifully are not, it appears – tuned in on the fringe of the most terrifying mental waveband of all. Great Cthulhu, dreaming but not dead, has for the past six days been sending out the most hellish mental nightmares from his House in R'lyeh. He has turned his wrath on all and everything. The weather, even for this time of the year, has never been quite so freakish,

188

the sudden virulent outbreaks of esoteric cult activities never more horrible, the troubles in insane asylums the world over never more numerous, and the suicide rate never so high. Sunspot activity has for the last two days been so bad that radio and television reception is worse than useless; meteorologists and other scientists in general have no answer for it. Last night top vulcanologists in four different countries issued warnings that at least seven volcanoes, four of them thought to have been long extinct and most of them many thousands of miles apart, are on the point of simultaneous eruption – 'Krakatoa will have been as a firecracker,' they warn. I admit to being terrified.

7th Dec.

Amazingly, this morning – after a night of tossing and turning, monstrous dreams, and morbid fear for the whole world's safety and sanity – all seems back to normal.

Later.

Crow has been around after receiving a trans-Atlantic telephone call from Peaslee explaining all. It was the buildup of Cthulhu's fury that decided Miskatonic's tele-pathic quintet – the same five which discovered the source of the trouble on its initiation a week ago – in their final course. Deliberately they set themselves against the Lord of R'lyeh, cutting in on his dream-sendings and matching their mental powers with his; and though (God-only-knows *how*) they seem to have done the trick, they've paid for their idiotic bravery in no uncertain fashion. They left a note for Peaslee, 'In case anything should go wrong!' Pityingly, but with no mean respect, the professor likens them to cabbages – alive, but only just, utterly mindless vegetable entities.

Following a lull in operations the Foundation seems to be back in full swing again. Crow and I have been offered status positions with Oil & Minerals International, an obscure but apparently well-financed mining and drilling concern – with headquarters in Arkham, Massachusetts! We have both declined these positions; Crow has his interests, I have my writing and my antique business to attend to; and besides, we know that Peaslee has many more irons in the fire, he in no way depends upon us. Specifically we were to have joined with other 'executives' of O & MI in Ankara, to organize what has been loosely termed 'The Turkey Operation'. We have agreed, however, to head Great Britain's Chapter of the Foundation here in England. Peaslee in turn has promised to keep us up-to-date on the state of things in Turkey. It should be most interesting; the frequency of severe Turkish earthquakes would seem to determine – quite apart from any dissertations on continuing continental drift or the widening of basic subterranean faults – that Turkey is literally crawling with Cthonians. In Titus Crow's own words: 'Well, it's a very nice offer, de Marigny, but discretion tells me that for the time being at least, we have done enough.'

5th Jan.

The last of the present series of French and American underground atomic tests have now been carried out, with more than merely military success I'm sure.

2nd Feb.

Peaslee, in a recent letter from Denizli, Turkey, informs us of the loss of a Foundation plane, its pilot, two crew members, and Hank Silberhutte. They were last heard of ten days ago somewhere in the Mackenzie Mountains, only a hundred miles or so south of the Arctic Circle. Silberhutte, it seems, has had a 'thing' about Ithaqua ('The Snow Thing', 'The Thing that Walks on the Wind', 'The Wendigo', etc.) of the Cthulhu Cycle, ever since a cousin of his vanished under mysterious circumstances in Manitoba some years back. In poor Wendy-Smith's time, too (during his *normal* lifetime, I mean), as witness his document and other credible contemporary papers, Spencer of Quebec University produced ample evidence of human sacrifice to Ithaqua by degenerate worshippers in Manitoba. Silberhutte was working on a long-term personal project of his, with the Foundation's blessing, to track this powerful air-elemental down. Peaslee believes that the telepath might have strayed – or been drawn – too far north, into the Wind Walker's domain; for it was to the Arctic regions that Ithaqua was banished for his part in the uprising of the Great Old Ones against the Elder Gods. Personally, I thank the Lord that I myself am not 'gifted' with any extraordinary degree of telepathic power.

11th Feb.

Crow has an interesting theory, one that can't be proved as yet but which certainly seems sound enough. Nyarlathotep, the Great Messenger of the Old Ones, the only prime member of the CCD left unchained by the Elder Gods at the unthinkably distant time of the prisoning, is not a being or deity as such at all but more truly a 'power'. Nyarlathotep is in fact Telepathy (Crow points out that the two words come quite close to being anagrammatical, but this must be purely coincidental), truly a 'Great Messenger', and certainly we know that the CCD do in fact communicate in this fashion. Of certain reported physical manifestations of Nyarlathotep, Crow says that he has little doubt that given the right type of mind to work upon the Great Old Ones could produce by telepathic means a very real tridimensional image – that such an image might even be in the form of a man!

15th Feb.

Following the initial success of the Turkey Project, Oil & Minerals International has secured contracts in Rhodesia and Botswana. Three of Pongo Jordan's most trusted and highly skilled engineering lieutenants, along with two of Peaslee's more experienced telepaths (in great demand now), are going out to Africa to organize the first stages of the operation.

28th Feb.

With the continuing success of the Apollo moon-shots comes disturbing news from Miskatonic. Along with all the other equipment deposited on the moon by America's epic adventurers were certain seismological instruments – and it now appears that Miskatonic's science laboratories had more than a small hand in the design of two of them! Quite apart from what NASA has learned of the moon's interior construction from such instruments, Miskatonic too has been 'listening in' – but for nothing so commonplace as moonquakes! The report has it that eventually it will be discovered that there is life *in* the moon; but by then (it is to be hoped) we will know just what that life is and how to deal with it. Could this be, I cannot help but conjecture, the source of those hellish radiations which, in their season, turn men's minds to those hideously aberrant acts that we classify as lunacy?

27th March.

In support of a letter from Peaslee received over a month ago – regarding the strengthening of the African force in an attempt to track down and extirpate Shudde-M'ell himself in his as yet undiscovered stronghold (G'harne is now deserted) – comes the following item, copied direct from yesterday's *Daily Mail*:

THE INNER-SPACE RACE!

Prior to the commencement of an Ethiopian 'Mohole' project, planned for a time some years in the future, the United States of America's Miskatonic University has jumped the gun on the British-led team at present carrying out survey work from Addis Ababa. There, below the tremendously hostile Danakil Desert where temperatures have been known to exceed more than 138° Fahrenheit in the shade, the three greatest rifts or natural faults in the Earth's crust meet, and it is there that the British scientists hope to bore a hole right through the crust to the never before pierced mantle.

This is not the first time that such a titanic feat has been attempted – the Americans have already known one failure in the Pacific Ocean near Hawaii in 1966. On that occasion the project was abandoned because of escalating costs. Similarly the Russians were defeated in the Arctic Circle's Koda Peninsula. But quite apart from depleted funds both projects met, too, with immense technical difficulties.

Professor Norman Ward, however, head of the Geology Department of Medham University and chief adviser to the British project's sponsoring authorities, seems unconcerned by the advent of the American group on the scene. 'They are way out in their calculations,' he says, 'if they believe that they have found the ideal spot in or near the area where they are at present encamped. The Afar Depression,' he goes on to explain, 'is far more suitable as a site for the project, but for some reason the Americans have chosen a spot well out of the way; and from what I have seen of their equipment – unless they intend to use previously untried methods – then I give them little chance of success. They are, though, a closemouthed lot, and I am given to suspicions that they have far more in mind than they let on.'

'Far more in mind than they let on,' indeed! Of course they have! They're after one of the biggest horrors the world has ever known – an incalculable evil which only

193

Great Cthulhu himself might surpass. I wish them luck, but I'm surely glad I'm out of it.

10th April.

Crow has been round about a communication from the Wilmarth Foundation. The Ethiopian thing is well under way and the three Foundation telepaths out there believe that they've found what they were looking for – Shudde-M'ell himself! They have, too, devised a 'lure' for that supreme burrower – a number of fresh-hatched and presumably very precious (ugh!) females – and with his awful tribe so depleted over this last year or so it's believed the horror *must* make a bid for the release of these would-be nest-mothers. There is one well, a shaft three-quarters of a mile deep, and down this shaft in four days' time the females will be lowered – along with an explosive device set to disseminate a mass of one of the most deadly radioactive materials known to science. Experiments at Miskatonic have already shown that materials of only one-tenth of the radioactive potency of the stuff will kill a normal (normal?) Cthonian. This could well mean the end of one of the greatest CCD.

15th April.

Disaster! Horror! The newspapers are full of it; but as of yet, no official word from Peaslee or the Foundation. Severe earthquake near Addis Ababa and tremors in the surrounding towns and villages – Miskatonic's entire Ethiopian team, all bar one man who managed to get away in a blazing vehicle – *wiped out!* The man who got away (no particulars yet) is on the danger list in an Addis Ababa hospital. Severe burns and shock. The story of what really happened hinges on whether or not he survives.

194

I have read Professor Ward's appraisal in the *Mail*; he appears to be of the amazed opinion that the Americans succeeded in their attempt to break through the Earth's crust, and that in so doing they somehow released the lava-stream which so far has obstructed all attempts by observers to get into the immediate vicinity of the site. He says that from the air the site is now a great molten crater a mile across – a crater with a slightly raised rim through gaps in which a lot of lava has escaped. All 'volcanic' activity has now stopped, apparently, but the place is still too hot to approach on foot or by surface vehicle. There is not the slightest sign or trace of the men who inhabited the place only a few short hours ago, and of the machinery they used only a metal spar from the great derrick itself has been found – hundreds of yards *outside* the northern rim of the crater, where it was presumably thrown by the force of the short-lived 'eruption'. Ward considers that he was correct in his initial theory – that the Americans were trying out new, quick-drilling methods – for this would seem the only satisfactory explanation for so rapid and disastrous a penetration of the Earth's crust. My God, if he only knew the truth! I imagine Miskatonic will soon put out a cover story.

2nd Aug.

My collection and correlation, over the last quarter or so, of my own notes and some of Crow's papers and documents into a record of sorts (as suggested by Peaslee some time ago) regarding our experiences with the burrowers beneath, has left me precious little time to spare; but I have managed to keep in touch with Crow himself, and with the Wilmarth Foundation. The receipt of occasional communiqués from America has helped to keep me fairly well up-to-date, despite the fact that I am no longer personally involved – or at best only partly involved, and then only in the now limited administrational duties of the organization's British Chapter. I cannot help but wonder, though, how long this anonymity of mine can last. Crow is at present in Oklahoma, and his letters hint of suspected subterranean wonders the lure of which I cannot hope to resist for long. He talks about 'embarking upon the greatest speleological expedition in history', but as yet has not explained himself. Now what in heaven . . . ? Potholing – ?

In the meantime the members of Miskatonic's august, inspired, and dedicated body abroad are making great strides in their concentrated efforts to track down and exterminate the remaining lesser agents and minions of the CCD. It seems generally recognized now that the greater of these horrors – such as the space-spawn of Cthulhu, Yibb-Tstll, Yog-Sothoth, Ithaqua, Hastur, and some half dozen others; notably the Lloigor, whose disembodied subterranean race-mind is still apparently exercised and felt most strongly in Wales – are here to stay; at least until our growing knowledge of them permits us a safe attempt at their expulsion. Their destruction, an actual *end* to them, now seems out of the question; if they were ever capable of being destroyed, then why were such merciful executions not undertaken by the Elder Gods themselves aeons ago? This, at any rate, is a question which Miskatonic's theorists have now started to chew over.

13th Aug.

In relation to my last entry regarding the CCD: whether or not *all* the greater beings are immortal may never be known – but Shudde-M'ell, at least, has shown himself to be almost indestructible! This has come out following the recovery of Edward Ellis, the sole survivor of the Ethiopian horror. Fortunately Ellis is – or *was* – a telepath, the most accomplished of the ill-fated trio sent out from America to Addis Ababa, and now that his extensive skin-graft operations and general therapy (mental as well as physical) are over and he is back on his feet, he has finally managed to tell what happened when the Prime Burrower went to the rescue of his doomed little females. He has confirmed beyond any reasonable doubt that those female creatures died in the incredibly destructive blast of hard radiation released by the present explosive device – but their lord . . . ?

Through the lull left by the instant shutting off of infant Cthonian thoughts, the telepath had picked up – had been almost blasted by – the most fearful waves of angered and agonized telepathic sendings as Shudde-M'ell reacted to the hard radiation. Wounded that great abomination may well have been, indeed Ellis' continued evidence guarantees it, but at the last – as witness the complete destruction of the well-shaft trap and of the men who set and baited it – he was very much alive!

I say that Ellis has told what happened when Shudde-M'ell surfaced, but I realize now that I may have given the wrong impression. As a telepath Edward Ellis is finished (it is a wonder they managed to save his sanity, let alone his telepathic powers), but he gave up what he knew of the thing under the inducement of certain special drugs taken voluntarily.

I have listened to copies of tape recordings made while Ellis was under the influence of those drugs. He babbles pitifully of 'a great grey thing a mile long chanting and exuding strange acids . . . charging through the depths of the earth at a fantastic speed, in a dreadful fury . . . melting basaltic rocks like butter under a blowtorch!' He gibbers of the explosion which released what ought to have been radiations ultimately inimical, indeed deadly to all known forms of life – particularly Cthonian life – and of the instantaneous blotting out of the mind-patterns of the young female creatures. He gabbles almost inarticulately of the injured, partly dissolved monstrosity which yet lived to bore its way to the surface, to turn its massive storehouse of heat and alien energy loose in a frenzy of molten destruction! Finally he sobs weakly of the horror's retreat, of its crash dive straight down into the bowels of the earth, until it achieved that which man still has not accomplished. For Ellis' mind was *with* Shudde-M'ell when, in blind agony and indescribable rage, the Prime Burrower *broke through the crust of the Earth – broke through to swim away deeper yet, into the inner magma, against strange tides of molten-rock oceans, those oceans which hold these lily pads we call continents afloat!*

There it was that Ellis lost the horror's trail, and there too he lost consciousness, but not before he managed to throw himself from his careening, blazing vehicle into the lifesaving waters of an oasis pool.

24th Aug.

Crow is coming home again to England!

It will be good to see him again – it will be good to *talk* to him! He has written to me of things almost beyond imagination: subterranean horrors totally outside man's sphere of knowledge, even beyond the combined ken of the Wilmarth Foundation, existing in the bowels of the earth beneath Oklahoma. His writing includes mention of the 'blue-litten world of K'n-yan', of the 'Vaults of Zin', of monstrous ruins of eldritch civilizations in a still deeper 'red-litten world of Yoth', and of undisclosed but apparently indisputable evidence in respect of his theories (and the Foundation's) regarding the unbelievable antiquity of the Cthulhu, Yog, and Tsathogguan Cycles of myth, legend, and cult. Finally he has hinted awesomely of the deepest abyss of all, 'Black N'kai, whose singular stone troughs and burrows are sufficient in their very *ancientness* to turn the minds of men away shrieking!'

I gather that no speleological expedition has actually been undertaken as was originally planned, and that all these allusions have their origin in telepathically inspired dreams; but knowing something of the workings of the telepathic mind I now find myself asking a terrifying question: if these places are so fearfully deep underground – *through what mental eye have such visions been relayed to the surface . . . ?*

But at any rate, the whole thing has been seen as far too dangerous for earnest investigation – certain Indian legends of unguessed lineage have come down through time; more recently, other serious investigators have met with strange disappearances and weird displacements of time and matter – and so massive charges of dynamite have been used to seal off these buried places for ever from our sane upper world. The horrors of K'n-yan, Yoth, N'kai, and kindred vaults are not truly of the magnitude of those we within the Foundation are pledged to fight – but they are still far too terrible to contemplate or correlate within a so-called rationally ordered universe.

29th Aug.

A letter from Peaslee: he asks if I would care to join him in co-leadership of an Australian 'expedition'. There are, he says, certain things in the Great Sandy Desert in which he has a very special interest. I know that he once accompanied his father out there back in 1935, and I believe he later published a very limited edition regarding some odd discoveries; but in any case I have had to turn him down. My antique business demands I take a hand here in England, and I still have certain administrational duties in respect of the Foundation's British Chapter.

3rd Sept.

Crow gets into London airport some time this evening. His last letter, received yesterday, is full of excitement; something to do with his discovery at Miskatonic University of a book containing fragments in an ancient glyph with corresponding paragraphs in Latin. He mentions his great old clock (that weird, four-handed, chronologically impossible monstrosity which once belonged to my father), relating the fantastic configurations on its dial to this latest 'Rosetta Stone' discovery of his. It's plain he believes that he can now decipher the legend of the clock, perhaps even discover the thing's purpose, for I've known for some time that he thinks the clock is in fact a space-time machine – a device come down from predawn days of extra-dimensional 'magic' – literally a toy of the Elder Gods themselves, or of others like them.

Crow's excitement, his prescience in this matter, is hardly unfounded. I recall something he told me some years ago, or rather something at which he hinted, about a pair of burglars who broke into Blowne House one night – and who stayed! Apparently one of these gentlemen-of-the-night found a way to open the clock, something Crow had never managed to do on his own, but thereafter my friend's story was vague indeed. I recall him saying something about frightening dimensions, 'a gateway to hideous times and spaces', and his mention of 'a lake of elder horror, where nightmare entities splash by a cloud-wave shore as twin suns sink in distant mists . . .' I must remember to have him relate the story in full. I'm sure he mentioned something about his 'visitors' *vanishing into* the clock! But there again, as I recall it, he was very reticent about the whole thing. In those days, though, we hadn't shared so many horrors.

There are other reasons, too, whereby Crow might just prove himself correct regarding the clock's purpose and origin. I can still remember – though I was just a lad at the time, living away from my father – a curious affair involving an East Indian mystic; one Swami Chandraputra, I believe his name was, who also disappeared in strange circumstances connected with the clock. Titus Crow has researched all this and knows far more of such matters than me. It will be interesting to see just what he has dug up.

14

Winds of Darkness

H. L. de M.
11 The Cottages
Seaton Carew, Co. Durham
28th September

Blowne House

Dear Titus,

Just a note to explain my absence should you try to contact me at home. I've been up here three days now, staying with friends, trying to recover from a rather severe attack of 'The Morbids'. It was quite sudden – I simply decided one morning (Tuesday last) to get out of London for a bit. The fog and all depresses me. Not that it's much better up here; the mist comes rolling off a sullen, dirty sea and . . . I don't know . . . I seem to be more depressed than ever. I've had some funny thoughts about this mood of mine, I don't mind telling you, though Britain is surely safe now – but in any case, I have my star-stone with me. I tried to talk to you before I left, but your telephone was out of order. I also tried calling you from up here, but – same story.

I got your note before I left, though, and I'm delighted you're finally cracking the code on that old clock of yours. I expect that by now you've just about got it beaten . . . ?

Damned annoying thing, but Sunday night before I came up north I had a burglar! God-only-knows what he was after, but he gets full marks for stealth; quiet as a mouse! Took a few pounds, but I couldn't discover anything else to be missing.

I think I shall probably stay here for a fortnight; perhaps I'll take a run up to Newcastle next week and see how old Chatham's antique shop is going. Last I heard he was doing quite well for himself.

All for now; do drop me a line when you get the chance –

Henri

Blowne House
1st October

Henri-Laurent de Marigny, Esq.
11 The Cottages
Seaton Carew

Dear Henri,

Your note is in; I'm pleased we're in touch again. Yes, my phone *is* on the blink – damned destructive hooligans, I should think! No sooner do I get the thing repaired than it's *kaput* again!

Strange that you should mention this depression of yours – I, too, have been feeling a bit under the weather – and what a coincidence, for I have also had a burglar! Same night as yours, too. There seems to be a glut of criminals in the city nowadays.

Regarding that old 'clock' of your father's: I have, as you say, 'cracked it', I've got it beaten. It's tremendously exciting! Night before last I actually *opened* the thing on my own for the first time. The whole front of the frame swings open on some principle of motion previously outside my knowledge, beyond human technology. There are no hinges, no pivots, and when it's closed there's not even a crack to show where a door might be! But that aside: if I'm correct, the clock will prove to be *literally* a door on fantastic worlds of wonder – whole worlds! – past, present, and future, to the very corners of space and time. The problem will be, of course, in controlling the thing. I am in the position of a Neanderthal studying the operational handbook of a passenger-carrying aircraft – except I have no handbook! Well, perhaps not *so* extreme, but it's difficult enough by any standard.

Had a letter from Mother Quarry – apparently she's had one of her 'visions'; says we're both in terrible danger, you and I. I'd say she's just a bit late, wouldn't you? But she's a dear really, and I often put a lot of faith in what she says.

On your proposed trip up to Newcastle: there's always the chance (remote I'll admit) that Chatham has mangaged to find some stuff I asked him to look out for long ago, especially certain very old textbooks that Walmsley mentions in his *Notes on Deciphering Codes, Cryptograms, and Ancient Inscriptions*. I'd be obliged if you'd check this out for me.

Yes, a trip sounds a good idea – I find I've a bit of a wanderlust on myself. I think I might take the car over to have a look at Stonehenge or Silbury Hill; I always find the contemplation of such monolithic relics calming somehow – though just why I shouldn't be calm is hard to say. Nevertheless, as I said before, it's true that I haven't been feeling my best of late.

All for now; best, as always,
T.C.

PS URGENT!

Henri: drop everything and get back down to London as quickly as you can. We're both either blind or daft – or both! WE'VE BEEN GOT AT, the two of us, and it's a race against time now. I haven't the time to write more, and telephoning now will be no use for there are powers ranged against us. I must catch the post and then I'll have to be at the renewal of my protections. Oh, and you can throw away that damned 'star-stone' of yours! I'll explain all when I see you, but WASTE NO TIME IN RETURNING TO LONDON!

T.C.

ADDENDUM

The foregoing fourteen chapters of this work (the last of which, Chapter 14, I have constructed myself from letters discovered in the ruins of Blowne House following London's 'freak storm' of 4th October) were penned and put together in their present order by Mr Henri-Laurent de Marigny, who introduces himself amply in the body of the work as the son of a great American mystic, as a collector and dealer in antiques, and lately as a member of the Wilmarth Foundation. The manuscript – complete apart from the preface, chapter titles, and headings, which I have appended for their obvious relevance – accompanied the letters in a locked metal box which Titus Crow had labelled and addressed to me.

The manuscript in its entirety should stand as an admirable if in parts sketchy record – to say nothing of a *warning* to present members of the Foundation – of de Marigny's and Crow's involvement prior to and following my first meeting with them (so amply chronicled), and their subsequent membership within the Foundation.

Strangely, I feel little concern over the apparent end of the affair; I have a feeling that for Crow and de Marigny it is *not* the end. As corroborative evidence in support of this feeling of mine, I offer the final note which Crow left for me in the metal box – a note which I found atop the other documents and manuscripts when the British police delivered the box to me earlier this year:

Peaslee, the storm gathers.

This note, I feel, will be brief – and I think I know which of the CCD has been given the final honour, that of removing de Marigny and myself from the surface of the Earth.

God, but Henri and I have been fools! You'll see from the two letters here that we had ample warning: the first feelings of increasing depression following those staged break-ins, 'burglaries' which served one and only one purpose, the removal of our protective star-stones and their replacement with useless duplicates; the unreasonable urgings to visit places which even Wendy-Smith had warned of as being dangerous since a time God-only-knows how long ago in the past – Stonehenge, Silbury Hill, Hadrian's Wall at Newcastle (you'll need to have another look at Britain, Peaslee!); the plan to split us up and deal with us separately, de Marigny up north and me in London. Oh, there's been enough of warnings!

I don't know how I tumbled it, really. I think it must have been Mother Quarry's letter of warning – and she was so right! How by all that's holy have they managed it, eh, Peaslee? How did they contrive to steal our star-stones? De Marigny thinks he has the answer, and possibly he's right. He reasons that our 'burglars' were not truly dupes of the CCD (or the Cthonians specifically), as we have come to understand such; that they were in fact genuine burglars, but that the CCD had implanted in each of their minds the merest germ of a notion to rob us – to steal the star-stones! The rest, of course, would be easy: typically weak-willed moronic types, such as we've already had to deal with, would have been used to deliver false, duplicate stones into the hands of the rather more clever criminals, possibly with some story or other to reinforce the previously implanted belief in the value of the real things. A further mental jab at the minds of these criminals and . . . and the rest would be up to them!

But whichever way it was done, Peaslee, the storm gathers now and I haven't much more time. I have renewed my protections around Blowne House – the Tikkoun Elixir, the chant against the Cthonians (the V. V. Incant.) and certain other 'occult' devices, but I know of no positive charm against *this*!

De Marigny is with me and we are facing the thing together. The storm rages outside; strange winds tear at the house and lightning flashes ever brighter. A few moments ago the radio

206

mentioned the 'local storm' on the outskirts of London. Good Grief, but they don't know the half of it!

It is Ithaqua, of course. Not the Wind Walker himself but his minions, elementals of the air, ranged against us from all corners of the sky. They mean to have us, Peaslee, make no mistake – and yet . . . there is a chance. It's a pretty slim chance, but one we may be forced to –

Not much time now, Wingate. Three times the house has been struck. I have seen trees ripped up by their roots from the garden. The howling is indescribably ferocious. The windows are being blown in one after the other. I hope to God old Harry Townley is saying one for us now! He should be able to see Blowne House from his place.

I tried to get around to the British Museum earlier; if I remember right you left a number of your star-stones there . . . ? But in any case, my car has been sabotaged – it's patent *They* still have their followers here in England, Wingate – and of course the phone is out of order again.

That last blast of lightning!

Shapes form beyond the broken windows . . . they are fighting to be in . . . de Marigny is solid as a rock . . . the clock stands open and greenly illumined from within . . . this is our way out, but God-only-knows where it may lead . . . Randolph Carter, grant I have the formulas right . . . don't despair, Wingate, and keep up the fight.

The roof –

My hopes for the two comrades are further bolstered by the fact that, despite the incredible extent of the damage to Blowne House, the bodies of the two were nowhere to be found in the ruins – which to me is hardly surprising. It only remains for me to say that during that 'freak storm' Crow's ancient clock seems likewise to have vanished; for no single trace of that – conveyance? – could be found, neither a splinter nor even the tiniest fragment; and I think I know what Crow meant when he wrote: '. . . this is our way out, but God-only-knows where it may lead . . .'

Wingate Peaslee
Miskatonic University
4th March 19–